The 13th Day of Christmas

JASON F. WRIGHT

SHADOW
MOUNTAIN

Visit us at ShadowMountain.com

Library of Congress Cataloging-in-Publication Data

Wright, Jason F., author.
  The 13th day of Christmas / Jason F. Wright.
       pages   cm
  Summary: When nine-year-old Charlee and eighty-one-year-old Marva are
both diagnosed with cancer, the prospects of having a merry Christmas seem
bleak. That is, until a series of letters and gifts that coincide with the 12 days of
Christmas begin appearing. And the last letter—for the 13th day of Christmas—
might just be the most important one of all.
  ISBN 978-1-60907-177-6 (hardbound : alk. paper)
  1. Christmas stories.   2. Cancer—Patients—Fiction.   I. Title.   II. Title:
Thirteenth day of Christmas.
  PS3623.R539A614 2012
  813'.6—dc23   2012025813

Printed in the United States of America
Worzalla Publishing Co., Stevens Point, WI

10   9   8   7   6   5   4   3   2   1

The 13th Day of Christmas

Other Books by Jason F. Wright

Christmas Jars
Christmas Jars Reunion
The Cross Gardener
The James Miracle
Penny's Christmas Jar Miracle
Recovering Charles
The Seventeen Second Miracle
The Wedding Letters
The Wednesday Letters

To the original Traveling Elf,
Willard Samuel Wright

Acknowledgments

No book makes it from an author's noggin to your hands without enormous assistance from talented teams of elves.

The Family Elves are led by my wife and favorite reader, Kodi. The others are Oakli, Jadi, Kason, Koleson, Pilgrim, Beverly, Sandi, Milo, Gayle, Sterling, Ann, Jeff, April, John, and Terilynne.

Early Reader Elves are Matt Birch, Michelle Denson, Rusty Ferguson, Stuart Freakley, Angie Godfrey, Josi Kilpack, Sandra Nazar, Laurie Paisley, Melissa Skinner, and Patricia Utley.

Professional Elves are Sheri Dew, publisher; Chris Schoebinger and Heidi Taylor, product directors; and the many other talented elves at Shadow Mountain. I'm also grateful for the family of elves at the *Deseret News* who challenge me each week to become a better wordsmith. They are Emily Eyring, Christine Rappleye, Aaron Shill, and Bob Walsh.

A special army of Christmas Elves earns thanks as the pioneer supporters of a very important cause: The Christmas Jars Foundation. They are Matt and Christa Birch, Keith and Sheri Bird, Les and Cynthia Blades, Aaron and Jessica Blight, Bruce "Duke" Brubaker III, Tamara Brubaker, Bruce "Brock" Brubaker IV, Brody Lee Brubaker, Gwen Casteel, Lynnda Robinson Coyle, Christie D'Amour, Margaret Dansie, Chad Decker, Cathy Ellis, Eric and Randa Farnsworth, Chrissy and Stephen Funk, Michael and Tanya Groll, Roberta M. Hulse, Kib and Lisa Jensen, Jeff and Lucy Kimble, Aaron and Jeanette Lee, Sarah Lovesee, Marcie Siegel McCauley, Lisa Mikitarian, Sandra Nazar, Laurie Paisley, Bob and Michelle Rimel, Shannon Rolfe, Mike and Sabrina Showalter, Michael Stephenson, Lisa J. Sullivan, Dan and Cindy Walsh, Tiffany Warner, and Mark and Margaret Wright.

Finally, sincere thanks to those of you who will become Traveling Elves and flip the pages of this book until they turn into action. This year, may each of us share our faith and celebrate the real meaning of the 13th Day of Christmas.

1
Marva

Marva Ferguson draped a wet yellow apron over the clothesline that ran along the side of her home. In curly cursive, a screen-printed message on the front of the apron boasted: *If life gives you lemons, throw them through the candy shop window and grab some taffy.*

It was just one of more than 150 aprons in the collection that hung ten deep on pegs and hooks around Marva's kitchen, pantry, and sunroom. She wore aprons while cooking, cleaning, and doing the laundry, and often changed them during the course of the day to suit her mood. It was hard to pick a favorite when she wore most of them only a few times each year, but this particular apron was a contender.

Marva knew she was probably the last person in the town of Woodbrook who still used a clothesline. Once, when local newspaper columnist Rusty Cleveland of *The Woodbrook Weekly* knocked on her front door asking to do a profile on her as part of a weekly *Know Your Neighbors* series, Marva agreed on the condition he help her hang the morning's load. Rusty had such a good time, he'd stopped by every couple of months since to check on the widow and work the clothesline. He'd even donated a few aprons to her collection.

She enjoyed Rusty's company and was grateful for his visits. She also appreciated the occasional drop-ins from the circle of widow friends she'd made at various volunteer gigs around town. But they surely didn't make up for the mornings when her husband, John, used to hang clothes with her. He'd been gone thirty-three years, but she still saw him in the next row, smiling over a pair of overalls or damp dishtowels.

John and Marva had an unusual history with laundry. When they were young, John joked with his pals that the first time he saw Marva, she was taking her clothes off. When their jaws dropped, he finished the joke. "Off the clothesline—get your minds outta the gutter!"

It was true.

She'd first laid eyes on him in 1946 while clipping a sand-colored beach towel to a clothesline in the backyard of her parents' home. The eighteen-year-old young man with bad hearing and a World War II deferment had been cutting her neighbor's lawn all morning, pushing a mower over the same patch of scratchy grass over and over like a perfectionist barber corralling a cowlick.

But the drunken snail's pace had nothing to do with lawn care. He just wanted to sneak peeks at Marva and admire the tall, sixteen-year-old with fire-red hair and a matching personality. He finally found the courage to introduce himself, but instead of the more formal introduction called for in 1940s America, he chose to pop up from behind a bedsheet with clothespins pinned to his ears and nose.

How could she not love the boy?

They were married five years later and spent many hours at the clothesline together until the second of two heart attacks took him in 1978. In the years since, she'd had plenty of suitors and had even been to dinner, the movies, or square dancing with a gentleman or two, but she never seriously considered remarrying. In her stubbornness, she determined that no other man's clothes were worth washing besides John Ferguson's. And there certainly were no other men she wanted to hang clothes with in the virgin morning air.

She told friends that even before she met him, there was only John.

When they were married, there was only John.

Now that he waited in heaven, there would be only John. And she was sure he would still want to do laundry with her.

Marva loved living life by hand, but it's not as if she'd never tried using a dryer. In 1961, John was inspired by outgoing First Lady and pink devotee Mamie Eisenhower and surprised his wife with a Frigidaire Pink Custom Imperial Washer Dryer set for their ten-year anniversary. She liked it just fine, and it saved time as advertised, but she missed the moments the couple spent in the yard peering at one another between cotton dress shirts and sundresses. The first time the dryer needed repair, Marva told John not to bother.

"I can live with the washer, John. It gets clothes cleaner than I ever could on the old board. But no dryer can get the clothes any cleaner on the line than God Himself. Plus, I think He makes them smell better."

John didn't argue.

Marva breathed in the morning air and admired her two lines of clothes, sheets, towels, and the lemon apron she'd chosen for the day. September had soaked up the southern humidity, and Marva thought the air had an unusual, tasty crispness to it, like a long, salted pretzel rod snapped in half.

She dove her hands into the pockets of her apron that read *(Insert Funny Apronism Here).* A few children played in the field that separated her house from the 27 Homes trailer park. She watched them for a long time as they played tag and built an obstacle course from old plastic trash cans and worn truck tires. She hoped when the sun gave up for the day, they'd each get a full meal and fall asleep with full bellies. She knew some would; some wouldn't.

Even after seeing generations of children come and go from the neighborhood, even though she'd looked hundreds of kids in the eyes as they bounced by her on their pogo sticks or rolled past on roller skates, she still wished each one were the grand-child she never had from the son who'd preceded her husband to heaven too early.

She watched until the kids in the field disappeared from view, and soon their distant laughter and shouts slipped away, too.

The trailer park hadn't always been named 27 Homes. When John and Marva sold the land to the town of Woodbrook, the planning commission proposed a low-income trailer park with twenty-one mobile homes on larger-than-average lots. The homes would go first to families with children, then the disabled, then veterans, then the elderly. The town billed the mini-development as a path to homeownership for those in need of a boost. It was a model Woodbrook hoped the surrounding county and other nearby cities and towns would adopt.

It didn't take long before Woodbrook squeezed in three more trailers and renamed it 24 Homes, complete with a new sign. Then, in 2001, they renamed it again, adding three nice double-wide trailers close to the entrance off the rural highway.

When the third sign went up, the town manager finally had the foresight to design the numbers so they could easily be removed if the mobile home park grew yet again.

Marva wondered what her husband would think of the neighborhood today. The place had been maintained for a decade, and the families worked hard to convey the impression that their trailers were not just temporary housing but permanent, comfortable homes. Yet, of late, many of the lots had taken ill. Most of the homes had faded siding; some were missing it entirely. A few homes still had nicely manicured lawns, but the majority of her neighbors had let their yards grow into jungles of weeds and broken swing sets.

She assumed the best in people though, and chose to believe the struggling families simply didn't have the energy to provide for their loved ones *and* care for the small plots of earth around them that they didn't even own.

She thought because the town owned the homes, residents certainly couldn't be expected to invest much in them. Once upon a time, she'd heard that 27 Homes had a waiting list. Now she wondered how many people thought of it more like a prison than a path to homeownership. Because the sputtering economy and job market had played no favorites, she'd heard that out-of-work tenants were often behind and negotiating to stay another month, then another and another.

Marva often said that selling the land was the smartest thing John had ever done, though he'd had his doubts. The deal allowed the Fergusons to stay on a large parcel at the northeast corner of the trailer park at the end of the main drive. Their home, once hidden like a juicy Southern secret in a grove of box elder trees, was now partially visible from a busy two-lane, east-west road that cut the county in half.

Still, more than three decades after his death, Marva was grateful to live in the only home they'd shared together and to know she'd likely die in it too, just as John had. John's decision to give up a portion of their land and privacy had become her nest egg when he left the world seven years before the law of averages and medical spreadsheets said he would.

The town had originally designed an entrance to the neighborhood that was large and inviting, with fat azalea bushes on either side and the 21, then 24, then 27 Homes sign framed by hydrangeas. The road in was straight and wide with plenty of room for bicycles, Big Wheels, and minivans. After fifty yards of mobile homes on both sides of the road, a short stem shot to the left with six more homes, three on each side of the street. Another handful of homes sat back on the main straight road before the street took a sweeping round right and dead-ended at Marva's private driveway.

Locals said the neighborhood resembled a fishhook and over time referred to the three sections as if they were parts of a real hook. The long main street in was called the shank, the short dead-end street was the barb, and the bend was the big turn that held another six trailers and led to the Fergusons' home.

Those in the trailers nearest the entrance rarely saw Marva anyplace except in her Mazda Miata as she zipped in and out. Though the town had agreed to cut and pave a separate entrance through the trees for the Fergusons to access their property, there had been so many excuses through the years that Marva and John had finally given up the fight. Plus, with John gone at the age of fifty, not long after the town closed the deal for the land and trailers began appearing, Marva found she didn't mind driving past the mobile homes and the children who occupied them.

Even though they rarely spoke to her, and more than one child had been caught hanging from her clothesline or stealing aprons for a laugh, their simple presence in her daily universe reminded her that she was not alone.

2
A Girl Named Charlee

Hey, Charlee Chew, have I ever told you the story about the monkey named Mason who jumped from the back of an airplane with a banana-shaped parachute?"

Charlee loved that her father's bedtime stories always began with a question. "You've told me lots of stories about Mason," she giggled her answer. "But not that one."

Mason had survived buckets of wild adventures at the hands of Thomas Alexander's colorful storytelling. He had defeated ninjas using lasagna noodles, built a riverboat from orange peels, and ran successfully for president of Monkeymerica. In one of Charlee's favorites, Mason went hunting in the jungle with a bamboo marshmallow shooter that only shot the extra plump kind used for making s'mores.

There were some nights, if Charlee got to bed on time,

when her father would tell a second Mason story with even more delicious monkey hijinks than the first. Charlee's mother said that her husband enjoyed telling the tales so much, he'd wind up telling them to an empty room when his daughter was grown and gone.

Charlee remembered the first night the color of the stories began to change. She'd been surprised when her father revealed that Mason's family was moving. Mason's monkey dad had lost his business and needed to find a different job in a different town. As he unfolded the tale, Charlee thought Mason's voice sounded a lot like her dad's. Soon many of the stories sounded a lot like his, too.

Mason's dad lost his business.

Mason's older brother needed to try a new school.

An angry chimpanzee from the bank was coming to take their house, and they had to find a smaller one.

Charlee watched her dad's eyes as he told the stories until they drifted away from hers and all she could see was the side of his tired face. It was wrinkled and leathery and looked like the purse her mother bought on vacation in Mexico. Charlee's dad had deep lines in his neck that got a little bit deeper and a little bit longer with every new story.

Then, one night, he was just too tired to stay for a story. He apologized, kissed her on the forehead, and looked at her much longer than usual. Charlee took her small hands and ran her fingers along the edge of his face and pinched his chin with both her thumbs. She thought he might smile, but he didn't. It only made him look away again, and she noticed that the lines on his neck were starting to look like frowns.

She thought nobody should have that many frowns.

Charlee soon noticed that when the stories went away, boxes began to appear in their place. Boxes of a hundred shapes and sizes started filling up and were stacked in big box towers in every corner of the house. Charlee's mother wrote in fat, black marker on the side:

Charlee's Clothes
Zach's Books
Dad's Files
Mom's Journals

One night after the box towers started, Charlee's dad entered her room when he thought she was already asleep. He took a stuffed monkey that still had the stiff paper price tag clipped to it and snuggled it next to her. He lifted her arm and squeezed the monkey underneath her left elbow.

She wanted to open her eyes and surprise him, to say thank you and give him a kiss before he could shut the door and let the room fall back into darkness. But even a child can tell when a mother or father is feeling sad.

He quietly offered that he'd bought the monkey weeks earlier and was going to give it to her for Christmas. But he'd decided Charlee might like it early to help get ready for their trip and fresh start.

When her father shut the door, Charlee flipped on the

lamp next to her bed and sat up to meet her new friend. He had long arms and longer legs that were well out of proportion with the rest of his body. He also had Oreo-sized eyes and a huge white smile that made her smile back because she knew his teeth were bigger than the teeth of any real monkey in the wild.

She hugged him tight, turned off the lamp, and for a long time wondered what to name her new monkey friend. But since she knew everyone assumed she'd name him Mason, she named him Melvin, instead.

"You deserve a fresh start, too," she whispered.

Less than one month later, Charlee was turned around in the clunky family minivan and hanging on to her seat's headrest, watching her old home in her old life become smaller and smaller. She watched until it was hidden under a smudge on the rear window. It felt like her entire life had been reduced to a speck so small it was hidden by dirt.

Before they crossed the county line, Charlee and Melvin were already tired of their brother Zach's grumbling from the third-row backseat. Zach rotated through a dozen complaints: "Why do we have to move so far away? Why did you sell my bike? I paid for part of that, you know. How much further do we have to go? I hated that stupid school anyway."

Zach and Charlee's mother, Emily, muted her son with threats of stopping the car, selling his two remaining possessions of value—an Xbox and an iPod—and making him start his new school immediately without the week off she'd promised the kids could have in order to settle in to their new life.

Charlee stared at the U-Haul her father drove ahead of them in traffic. She wished she could have sat beside him instead of by her pouty brother. When they finally passed a sign that read *Welcome to Woodbrook—America's Friendliest Small Town*, Zach announced from the back of the van, "More like Welcome to Dumbbrook—America's Dumbest and Dinkiest Small Town."

Charlee told Melvin not to listen to her grouchy brother, and she covered the monkey's ears with his own long arms and hands. Then she looked out the window at the different trees, different road signs, and different neighborhoods and wondered if her little own life would be better, or just different like the scenery.

The longer she looked and the faster her mother drove, the more the strange sights outside her window began to merge and blur. The people on the street looked wet, stuck inside clouds so thick she couldn't tell if they were people anymore. It reminded her of diving underwater for coins at the old community pool and looking up at her dad's fuzzy figure standing on the edge.

"Mom, I have a headache," she said. "Can we stop?"

"Sorry, Charlee, we're not that far now. Dad's just stopping to pick up the keys. We'll be there soon. I promise."

Charlee took Melvin's furry hands and rubbed her own head with them. After another few minutes of navigating

Woodbrook's unfamiliar streets, Charlee's stomach began to churn, and she again asked to take a break.

"Please, Mom? I feel sick. Car sick."

"Quit being a baby," Zach shot from the backseat, and Charlee wondered how her brother had heard her through his earbuds and the screaming he called music.

"We're almost there. I know it's been a long drive, Charlee, but we're almost there. Maybe take your glasses off."

Charlee did and then closed her eyes, using Melvin as a pillow against the van window. Her mind slid from worry to worry like a smooth metal piece on a board game. Would the kids on their street be nice? Next space. Would she make new friends? Another space. She'd never changed schools before. Back two. Would she really make new friends? Skip three. Would her teachers treat her strangely? Would they speak too loudly or too slowly as if she came from some other country and spoke some other language? Would people find out her brother was kicked out of school? Would her dad's new job work out? Would their new house be big enough for everyone?

She opened her eyes and studied her reflection in the window. Her hair was black and straight and threatened to once again tickle her shoulders. Charlee had had much longer hair a few months earlier, but her mother cut it short at the beginning of the summer, and Charlee thought the cut made her look like a boy. She couldn't be sure whether that was her own opinion, or her mind parroting what other children had said too loudly when they didn't care if she overheard them.

Plus, Charlee didn't like boys yet, so why would she want to look like one? She was thankful that even though her hair had not yet completely recovered after the long summer, she was starting to look like a young lady again in the mirror.

Charlee's tired eyes were dark, too, but more warm chocolate brown than black. Her father called the color *Hershey's Kiss* and even wrote it that way on whatever school forms or paperwork required eye color identification. She'd worn cherry-red framed glasses for almost a year, but lately they gave her headaches. Her mother promised that once they were on their feet in their new place, they'd update the prescription.

It was only mid-afternoon, but her eyelids soon collapsed under the heavy weight of child-worry. In her dreams, she saw Zach knocking over moving-box towers in their old home and their mother following behind setting them back up.

Charlee didn't wake until Zach leaned forward and bopped her head with an empty Gatorade bottle. "We're there."

She sat up and rubbed her eyes, clearing the fog just in time to see her dad in the U-Haul take a wide left turn from the main road onto what looked like a neighborhood street. They followed him, and she noticed a wooden sign surrounded by overgrown bushes:

"Welcome to 27 Homes."

3
Welcome Home

Dad, you said it was a manufactured home, not some trashy trailer."

"Zachary—" his mother snapped.

"It's okay." Thomas took a step toward his son in the front yard of their new mobile home. "I should have prepared you better." He put a hand on Zach's shoulder.

"You think?" Zach said before dropping his shoulder from underneath his father's touch.

"We'll make the best of it—that's what we do, right, gang?" Thomas wasn't sure he believed it himself, but it was what he'd been repeating in his mind for hours while he was alone in the bouncy cab of the rented truck.

"That's right," Emily tried. "We'll make an adventure from this. It's a brand-new start for everyone."

"In that?" Zach said, gesturing with both hands, palms up, toward the double-wide trailer, as if wanting to lift it from its concrete slab foundation and make it taller.

"It will become what we make of it," Thomas said, but he knew instantly it was a cliché Zach would dismiss. "It's a clean slate, son. I know it's not a house with a big yard and a game room. But it's all we can afford right now. Honestly, Zach, we're lucky to even have it. My new boss pulled strings to get us this home—"

"Trailer," Zach interrupted.

"It's a trailer now," Emily said, "but when we get inside, we'll make it ours. We'll make it a home."

"And soon, if everything goes well, we'll find a bigger place," Thomas said. "We'll even let you help pick it out. How about that?"

"Right." Zach didn't say the word; he breathed it. Then he put his earbuds back in and walked toward the trailer.

"He'll be fine," Thomas said, and repeated it, more for himself than his wife. He manufactured a smile and asked Charlee to gather her things from the van. She disappeared into the van to repack her backpack.

Thomas nodded toward the U-Haul and silently invited his wife to follow.

"What do you think?" he asked as they leaned against the passenger's door of the truck's cab.

"It's about what I expected."

Thomas rested his arm on the large rearview mirror that was covered in bugs and dirt. "And that is?"

"Just what I expected. Just that. No better, no worse. It's what it looked like in the pictures you texted me."

"Huh. I hoped it would outperform those cruddy pictures, actually."

"It doesn't, if I'm being honest. But I can't say I had high hopes, either. I knew what we were getting into."

Thomas sighed and tried to fill his lungs with fresh, Saturday, anything-is-possible air. "I know it's not exactly like the website promised either."

"No, not exactly."

"But it's something."

"Yep, it's something all right." Thomas knew Emily meant it to be funny, but as actors in a scene neither wanted to be in, the line had an uncomfortable edge.

Emily took a beat, crossed her arms, and took her own deep breath. "It has potential, I suppose."

"Potential."

"Sure. Potential to be better than it is right now."

Thomas wondered if she was still referring to the new home or to something bigger. "I can live with that."

"It's going to be hard, you know," Emily said with her eyes fixed on Zach rummaging around an overturned trash barrel.

"I know."

They watched Zach throw gravel, one rock at a time, at a

tire-lined flowerbed. The pebbles bounced off and scattered in every direction without order or pattern.

"Do you think he'll make it?" Thomas asked without looking away from him.

"I hope so."

Zach stopped long enough to fiddle with his iPod and then resumed pelting the tire, seemingly amused by the dull sounds and unpredictability of the ricochet.

"Sometimes I think he's just a typical teenage boy, like all his friends. But some days I think it's worse. Like he really needs help, you know?" Emily looked at her husband and waited for agreement.

"He's just a normal kid, Em."

Emily gathered and tucked a disobedient rope of hair behind her ear. "Not all kids get suspended, let alone kicked out of school."

"Maybe not, but maybe this is exactly what he needs. Even if he doesn't know it. A chance to start over."

They were both still looking in Zach's direction, but neither really saw him anymore.

Thomas was remembering the first signs of trouble. They received a phone call reporting that Zach had teased a Hispanic student to tears during English class. The next call came a few weeks later, which led to a three-day suspension. Zach had made fun of a student for crying during P.E. and pushed another boy for trying to defend him. The pushing counted as a second offense, and combined with his original transgression meant the county's "Three Strikes, Three Days" bullying policy went into effect.

Zach survived the second semester, at least without any formal punishment, and had a long summer to think about how much more difficult high school would be. But before the new school year's waxy smell had faded from the gymnasium, before anyone had forgotten their locker combination or gotten a report card, Thomas and Emily received another phone call. Zach was suspended for soaking another student's biology textbook in a lab sink overnight.

Zach came home from school angry and stayed that way for days. When he wasn't grouching at his parents, he was so locked into his video games the house could have collapsed around him and he wouldn't have noticed until the power went out.

A week later, Thomas's one-man construction company had finally caved to a year of pressure and gone bankrupt. Calls for kitchen renovations and backyard decks were so rare he got more wrong number calls than new clients. Soon letters and voicemails from the bank came more frequently, as did calls from collections agents, the IRS, and the insurance provider. Thomas had angry suppliers, at least three customers with unfinished jobs, and one subcontractor threatening more than a lawsuit.

The misfortune collected over their heads like a violent weather system and wiped the Alexanders from the map. They'd been lifted from the community they'd loved and dropped in the town of Woodbrook—America's Friendliest Small Town.

Thomas looked at his watch and groaned. "We're late. We gotta get the truck back, or we pay another day."

Emily called to Zach and Charlee, who were now exploring the side yard and remnants of what looked like a garden. "Time to work, kids."

Thomas pulled the trailer keys from his pocket and held them out for Emily. "Welcome home?"

"Yes." She took the keys and steeled herself. "Welcome home."

4

Someone Always Sees You

Charlee sat on a rotting railroad tie and picked at weeds that fought for life through narrow black holes. They'd been in 27 Homes a week and she'd only met a few other children.

On Monday, a girl offered her a cigarette that she claimed to have stolen from the outside pocket of her uncle's fishing waders.

On Wednesday, a younger girl so shy she couldn't utter a word besides her first name approached Charlee. Filled with joy at having a conversation with someone besides her cranky brother, Charlee overreacted with a hundred questions; the girl turned around and slugged away.

"Nice meeting you," Charlee called out from behind, but she wasn't really sure if it qualified as a meeting or not.

On Thursday, a boy Zach's age noticed Charlee's white-and-pink Reebok's and asked if she was rich. When she didn't answer right away, he said, "That's what I thought, new girl," and sauntered off.

Charlee's mother kept her promise to give the kids a full week off before starting school. Her dad began work the Monday after they arrived, and Charlee hadn't seen him much since. He was gone when she woke up, and he didn't walk back in the door until almost bedtime. She didn't know exactly where he was working, just that a man picked him up every day and they drove to a warehouse where they picked up big sheets of rock and hung them in houses other people were building.

She'd asked for a story the night before when he poked his dusty head in her room at bedtime. He promised that when they were settled—"really, finally settled"—Mason's adventures would return.

After a week, Charlee thought she knew the neighborhood layout like she'd lived there forever. The trailers closest to the main road were the nicest, she'd noticed, and the people who lived in them drove the nicer cars that made less noise and spat less smoke when they drove by. *Their trailers also seem much wider,* she thought, and she imagined they must have looked like mini-palaces inside. The trailers by hers were just okay, not bad, and definitely nicer on the outside than the six that sat on the short dead-end road with the ugly dirt and gravel mountain at the end with grass growing from it. She'd seen kids playing King of the Hill there, and she watched from the road's entrance, standing bravely in the middle of the street, hoping they'd see her and invite her to watch or be a judge or a referee, but they hadn't.

The older people lived in the trailers along the big bend in the main road and they were friendlier. Three ladies at one of the trailers sat on a wooden deck a foot off the ground with no railings and rocked all day in the kind of rockers Charlee had seen at Cracker Barrel. They waved when she walked by, no matter how many times she'd passed by and no matter how much time had ticked by since her last appearance in their eye line.

Charlee spun around on the railroad tie and began plucking long dandelions from the ground. When she'd picked every one within reach, she stood and picked another nearby patch clean. Soon the bouquet was too big for her hand. She sorted through it, tossing the limp, fading ones to the ground and placing the longest and brightest dandelions in a line atop the railroad tie. The moment reminded her of her Grannie Alexander's funeral two summers earlier and, for just a second, she felt like an awkward mourner all over again.

She sat back down and remade her bouquet. Her mother had gone "to fill out applications," she'd said before she left. Zach was inside playing video games and hogging the only television they still owned. It was really a computer monitor, but her dad had found a way to watch television on it. He said that the previous family had paid for too many months on accident so the Alexanders would be getting free cable, whatever that meant.

Her father was working a different job. Her mom called it a side-job and said he would be working a lot of those on the weekends for a while. Charlee wished she had a side-job for him, too.

Charlee looked across the wide field behind their trailer and saw a sea of dandelions she figured would take a whole month to pick. The field grass was bushy and thick in spots and bald in others and looked like her old elementary school principal's head. On the far edge of the field, she noticed the woman with the sports car and the big house at the end of the street was outside at her clothesline.

She'd seen the woman before and waved at her whenever she drove by their trailer on her way out of the neighborhood. Charlee had asked her mother for permission to knock on her door and say hello, but her mom said no.

"Charlee Alexander, you do not, under any circumstances, have permission to knock on her door or any other door in this neighborhood. I worry enough that you walk up and down the road."

Charlee picked another handful of dandelions and inched toward the edge of their backyard until she found a perfectly flat tree stump. The podium made her look a foot taller and feel at least ten feet more important. She lifted the bouquet above her head, and with her other hand, she took off her glasses and put them over her heart. She closed her eyes and imagined herself winning a beauty pageant or an Olympic gold medal.

The early October weekend breeze stiffened, and she put

her glasses back on. When she could focus again, she saw that the old woman across the field had stopped to watch her. And though Charlee couldn't hear her, it looked like she was clapping.

She hopped off the award's podium and waved to the woman. The woman waved back in an exaggerated circle and Charlee waved again. The woman also waved her arm again, but this time the greeting turned into an invitation, and she seemed to be calling Charlee over.

Charlee jogged to her trailer and looked in a back window to the living room. Zach was exactly where he'd been an hour ago, sitting on a beanbag held together with duct tape and cradling an Xbox controller in his lap. She could have asked him for permission to cross the field, but lately Zach's favorite saying had become "Quit bothering me."

So she didn't.

She turned away from the window and crossed back through the yard toward the field. She stepped over a fallen fence that had been on the ground for so long, she thought parts of it looked stuck in the ground, as if the earth had gotten sick of supporting it and swallowed up the railings out of spite.

She began crossing the field, pausing to pick only the longest of the dandelions and adding them to her second bouquet. When she found one fuller than another, she tossed the imperfect flower aside and replaced it. Charlee promised herself that no matter what, when she got to the woman's yard, she would obey her mother and not knock on the woman's door if she went inside.

She prayed the woman wasn't thirsty or tired.

The clothesline woman had gone back to pulling clothes and setting them in a plastic basket. By the time Charlee reached the edge of the woman's own lawn, marked, she assumed, by big red stones that lay flat with the grass, the woman had nearly emptied the line.

Charlee stood on a stone and smiled at her. She was close enough now to read the woman's apron: *Make yourself at home! Please start with the dishes.*

Charlee smiled even bigger.

The woman smiled back.

"My name is Charlee Alexander."

"Hello, Charlee Alexander. My name is Marva Ferguson."

Charlee took a step forward. "Most people just call me Charlee."

Marva smiled again. "And most people call me Miss Marva."

Charlee took two more steps. "I like that."

"Me, too." Miss Marva took the wooden clothespins she'd been collecting in her apron and began pinning them back onto the thin rope line. Miss Marva held several out toward Charlee. "Would you like to help?"

Charlee nodded, set her bouquet down on one of the stones, and finished her slow approach. She arrived at Miss

Marva's side, took the pins from her, and pinched one onto the line.

"Have you ever done this before, Charlee?"

"No, ma'am. We've never had a clothesliner before."

Miss Marva giggled. "My. That's a shame, isn't it then."

"We've always had a dryer. Until now. We don't have a dryer anymore."

"You don't?" Miss Marva handed Charlee another handful of pins and motioned to the second of the three lines.

"We did have one. At our old house. We sold it at the yard sale."

"I see."

"Mom took our clothes to a laundry place last night. She said they had dryers there so we wouldn't need one of our own."

"Your mother sounds very smart," Miss Marva said.

"She's super smart."

The two new friends remained quiet a moment, and Charlee didn't notice that Miss Marva was removing pins already on the line with one hand, putting them in one pocket, transferring them to the other, and handing them to Charlee to replace on the line.

"How long have you been in Woodbrook?"

"Exactly one week. We moved in last Saturday."

"I see."

"Do you have kids?" Charlee asked after another short pause.

"I do. I have one. A son."

"Does he live here?"

Miss Marva grinned. "No, I'm afraid not. He lives there." She looked up to the sky and then back to meet Charlee's eyes.

"Heaven," Charlee said.

"That's right. You're super smart, too."

"Thank you. And I'm very, very sorry, Miss Marva."

"He's been there a long time, so don't you worry."

When Miss Marva moved to the third line, Charlee darted back to the row of red stones and reassembled the dandelion bouquet. She appeared in front of Miss Marva and extended the flowers. "These are for you—for your son."

Miss Marva dropped the remaining pins in one of her apron pockets and took the dandelions. Her voice cracked when she tried to speak, so instead she put the bouquet to her nose and inhaled deeply. Then she tried again. "They're just . . ." She smelled them once more. "They're just beautiful."

Charlee smiled and admired her work. *Miss Marva is right,* she thought. *They are beautiful.*

A comfortable quiet lasted several minutes as Miss Marva retrieved an oversized clothespin from one of the other lines and used it to bind her bouquet of dandelions. Charlee watched with curiosity as Miss Marva disappeared into the back door of her home and returned a minute later without the flowers.

Miss Marva and Charlee spent half an hour making a game of spacing the pins at exact intervals across all three lines. They chatted about Zach and the Alexanders' move to Woodbrook, and Miss Marva explained the letter J fishhook design of the neighborhood.

"So that's your home there?" Miss Marva pointed. "So you're on the main road in. That's the shank; that's what people here say. And the side road with the trailers and the dirt pile? That's the barb—you know, like on a fishing hook."

"Uh-huh."

"And I live here all by myself on the point. On the end of the hook."

Charlee couldn't wait to share the fishing map with her parents that night, and she hoped more than ever that her father would be home before bedtime.

Charlee shared what she'd learned about her neighbors so far, which wasn't much, and Miss Marva told her to be extra kind to the three ladies in the trailer on the bend in the hook.

"Two of them are quite sick," she said. "They don't have a lot of waves left in them."

Charlee confessed that she was feeling lonely in the neighborhood, and that despite her efforts, she felt as if the other kids didn't even see her.

"You shouldn't feel that way," Miss Marva said. "I'm sure they saw you."

Charlee shrugged, and, like a tank low on fuel, they both seemed to tire, sputter, and run out of things to say and clothespins to rearrange.

"You want to know a secret before you go?" Miss Marva leaned down.

"Sure!"

Miss Marva cupped her mouth with both hands and whispered in Charlee's ear. "Are you ready?"

"Uh-huh."

"Someone *always* sees you."

5
Whisper-Shouts

Thomas, didn't they promise to pay you before you left?"

"They did."

Charlee heard her mother's angry sigh through the thin wall between the room she shared with Zach and the almost toy-sized kitchen of their mobile home.

"You can't let them do this to you. If the deal is to pay the same day you work these side-jobs, then don't leave until they do."

"Em, it's not that simple." His voice was quieter than her mother's, but she still heard his whisper-shouts well enough to be sad they were fighting.

"Why take the jobs then? Why spend another day away from us doing extra work when you have to chase them for the money later? If you're not going to get paid, Thomas, I'd rather you not get paid and at least be home."

"You're getting a little loud," he said.

"I'm whispering, Thomas. And Zach's listening to music in bed, and Charlee is asleep."

Charlee heard nothing for a moment, and she wasn't sure if the whisper-shouts had become just whispers or if they'd stopped.

"I was going to tell her a story tonight," she finally heard her father say.

"I know."

Charlee listened as their conversation turned back to money, people they owed money, why they need money, what they'd do with money, and why her mother was having a hard time finding a job of her own. Charlee pulled Melvin close to her and arranged him so their heads shared the pillow and their eyes met. They stared at the bottom of Zach's bunk bed above them.

"Charlee asked me about Christmas today," her mother whispered.

Her father didn't answer right away, and when he did, his voice was so quiet Charlee could only guess at what he'd said. "She asked you about Christmas?"

"She did."

"But it's only October."

"I know it's only October. But you know Charlee—she

thinks, she worries about us, she's got that old soul. She looks down the road more than we do."

"And she loves the holidays."

"She does."

"So?"

"So what?"

"So what did you tell her about this year?"

"I told her we'd be fine. That's how I answer every question, Thomas. We'll be fine. You'll be fine. Zach's just angry today; he'll be fine. I'll be fine, just give me a few minutes. Your dad is really tired today, that's all. He'll be fine."

"That answer won't work forever," he said, probably louder than he meant to.

"You think I don't know that? Trust me. I know that better than anyone. I feel sick when I put that *fine* face on. It feels like a lie, Thomas."

"Emily—"

"Look at us. Just look at your kids. Zach is suffering. He's completely alone. This hasn't been a fresh start. He's the same kid, only more invisible. I don't even recognize him anymore. He's broken. Don't you see it? No one trusts him, and no one even pretends he exists. And Charlee? She's dying here, Thomas."

"Now come on. It's going to—"

"To what? Be fine? Will it? We're living in a shoe box in a town we don't know, with neighbors who barely speak to us and mostly treat us like we don't belong here. We're avoiding ten calls a day. No, *I'm* avoiding ten calls a day while you're working until you're so tired you roll in the door and fall asleep before I even know you're home, half the time. Me? I'm filling out applications to fast food places that make you wear a paper hat. Paper hats, Thomas. And you're working fourteen hours on a Saturday at some job site where you can't even collect the money they promised."

"That's not fair."

"Not fair? Is any of this fair? This life you've dropped us into?"

"Is this about *me* now, Emily?"

Charlee turned on her back in bed. She felt the tears in her head deciding where to go, and an ache began to build behind her eyes. She wanted to get up and get a drink, maybe ask her mother for some aspirin, but she didn't want them to think she'd heard their whisper-shouts.

"Isn't it about you? Isn't it about you and your big business plans? The truck? The gear? All the junk?"

"Junk?"

"The stuff, Thomas. The stuff that buried us."

"Emily—"

"You buried us, Thomas."

A minute passed with nothing, and to Charlee, it felt as long as the time it takes to give someone a hug. She hoped that was it.

Another minute passed, and then the door to the trailer

opened and slammed shut. Charlee leaned out of her bed to look up at Zach.

His earbuds were off, and his eyes were open. "What's your problem?" he said.

"Nothing."

"Go to sleep then."

"I'm not sleepy."

"I don't care. Go to sleep anyway. You're a kid."

Charlee paused. "You're a kid, too, Zach."

"Whatever. Just shut up and go to bed." Zach grunted. "I hate sharing a room with you."

Charlee stayed quiet a moment before saying, "We're not supposed to say shut up."

Zach's head appeared over the edge of the top bunk. His face was red and became redder as he hung sideways. "You going to go out there and tell, Charlee? You really think Mom and Dad care if I say shut up?"

When Charlee didn't answer quickly, Zach added a nasty, "Grow up, Charlee," and flipped back on his bunk with an exaggerated flop.

"No, why don't you grow up? You're so mad all the time! I hate it, and I hate how mean you are, and I hate sharing a room with you more."

Charlee knew she didn't mean it, but she decided not to say another word that night. Because she'd realized she was whisper-shouting, too.

6

Christmas Help Wanted

Marva awoke at 6:17 A.M. The alarm had been set at that odd time for so long she didn't even remember why anymore. But she didn't mind. Marva liked to be up early, and even though she'd been more tired lately and wearing down earlier in the day, waking up under the blue-black denim sky reminded her she was still alive and in control of her day.

She felt sorry for the elderly men and women she volunteered with at the town library and the nearby physical therapy clinic. Too many of them were giving in to the aches that whisper and gossiping about sore knees, hips, and lower backs. Sure, Marva looked over her shoulder and saw the pains gaining, following her wherever she went like a thief waiting to steal what she did not protect.

But she would not release her grip. The years would have

to threaten someone else; Marva Ferguson would not hear the taunts.

Marva sat up in bed and, just like every morning since the spring of 1970, she picked up the phone on the nightstand to listen for a dial tone to be assured it still worked. It did; it always had.

She showered slowly, then dressed and selected an apron from her collection to wear while she prepared breakfast. It read *Yes, I'm a superhero, and I'm fully aware my cape is on backwards.*

She ate two pieces of bacon, half a grapefruit, two eggs, and a toasted English muffin with blackberry jam. She knew it was a large meal for a woman her age living alone. But she also knew that the more time she spent at the table, the more time she had to read her Bible. She'd been reading during breakfast since her teen years, and the daily tradition had followed her into married life and on to being a widow.

Plus, Marva enjoyed the large meal because she planned to do a lot of living, and a hearty breakfast would fuel her through the early afternoon.

It was, after all, the day she planned to put up Christmas.

After washing her dishes, something she always did immediately following whatever meal she enjoyed, Marva opened the deep linen closet inside the guest bedroom at the end of the hall. She couldn't remember the last time the closet actually held linens, but that was all right because she couldn't remember the last time the guest bedroom held a guest, either.

She pulled out the faded, green canvas bag that protected

her artificial tree. Real trees were nice, but her late-sweetheart, John, had purchased this tree at Sears, and every time she put it up, it reminded her that he wasn't as far away as he sometimes seemed.

Then came boxes of traditional ornaments, lights of every kind, and several popcorn strings that hadn't been supplemented with fresh popcorn in far too long. There were also bows, tinsel, stars, miniature stockings, plastic candy canes, real candy canes that were so old they looked plastic, and a few of her favorite recipes shrunk and laminated into ornaments that hung from pieces of yarn strung through paper-punched holes.

Marva also pulled her nativity scene from the closet. As much as she loved the Santa side of Christmas, Marva knew they were just decorations on the spiritual tree. No string of lights could shine brighter than the nativity that represented the real meaning of the holiday.

Lastly, Marva retrieved the box her husband had made from a pallet and later lined with red felt. It held the unusual wooden Advent calendar that dominated her mantel from late October through December. She liked the looks she got on Halloween when sticky-faced trick-or-treaters peered inside her front door and saw her southern extension office of the North Pole.

There were years when her friends were too overbooked with family and parties to visit her dripping-with-the-holidays home. But putting up Christmas right before Halloween meant that no matter what, even on the lonely years, someone would appreciate her work. Even if it was only from the front door, and even if it was from someone holding a pillowcase of candy and dressed as a character from a horror movie.

Marva resisted the urge to start with the Advent calendar. It had been the last decoration to go up every single year, and every single year she'd almost given in and cheated the schedule. When John was alive, he'd playfully hide it under the bed or in the pantry and magically produce it only when the rest of the house was ready. She had no need to hide it anymore, and she carefully placed it on the corner of the kitchen counter until the time arrived. But she avoided looking at it, just to be safe.

Marva remembered the year John made it by hand. It was their first Christmas without their son, J.R., and she'd asked her husband to make the calendar for her as her only gift. John had been a successful door-to-door salesman most of their married life, and despite his legs burning and his shoulders aching, he spent time in his shop almost every night in November, perfecting the wooden case and handcrafting each compartment and door. He'd raced to finish it by December 1st and Marva wept when he presented it to her that morning.

Marva knew her tears were an odd mix of happiness and grief, but they didn't stop her from placing the Advent calendar on the mantel that morning and filling each compartment but the twenty-sixth with a gumdrop. The space behind Day 26 didn't get a gumdrop; it got something else.

John hadn't fully understood why she'd requested the calendar go one day longer than usual, to December 26, but Marva promised him that when Christmas arrived, it would be as clear as the Christmas star.

All her handling of the boxes and tree had left her breakfast apron dirty from the dust storm of impatience. It was time for a Christmas apron anyway, and she sorted through a dozen on a long peg in the pantry. She chose one with the image of a chunky elf popping the buttons on his red, green, and white outfit. A roll of pink belly flab hung over his belt, and he said in a speech bubble, *You can be Santa's little helper. I'll be the helper who likes pie.*

She tied on her apron by the kitchen window and smiled at the sight of Charlee standing on the stump at the edge of her family's backyard. It was just how she'd first seen her, except this time Charlee was trying to twirl like a ballerina on one foot. She never quite made the complete circle before losing her balance and hopping off.

Marva opened the back door and walked toward the stone walkway that separated the property she still owned from the spacious field between her and 27 Homes. She enjoyed a few more of Charlee's spins, some with her finger above her head, and when Charlee finally saw her, she jumped back on the stump and waved wildly with both arms, as if signaling for help across the sea from a tiny, deserted island.

Marva waved her over, and Charlee ran the opposite direction toward the trailer. A minute later she reappeared and sprinted halfway to Marva before stopping to catch her breath.

Marva laughed when Charlee began running again, but soon stopped to walk the rest of the way.

"You're quite the dancer," Marva said.

"I am?"

"Back there." Marva pointed to the stump.

"Oh, yeah . . . No, I'm not really very good. I can't even spin all the way around without getting dizzy."

"Well, you look quite talented to me."

Charlee smiled and a rush of blood turned her face pink. "Thank you, Miss Marva."

They chatted about the unseasonably warm weather, and Marva explained what the word *unseasonably* meant. Charlee asked if there was anything to hang on the line, and Marva explained that she was all caught up, but that she'd need help in the morning.

Charlee pointed at Marva's apron and giggled. "I get it," she said.

Marva winked. "How would you like to help me with something inside?"

"What?" Charlee asked with such enthusiasm that Marva heard only the *Yes!*

"You'd have to ask your parents first, but I could use some help with my Christmas decorations."

Charlee cocked her head to the side. "Christmas?"

"I know, the calendar says October, but my house will say December by the time the sun sets."

Charlee held her chin. "Will you excuse me?"

Marva didn't have time to answer, giggle, or argue because Charlee was galloping back across the field of scattered dandelion bunches toward her trailer. Once again, she started and stopped several times, and Marva admired her tenacity. When the door to Charlee's trailer shut behind her, Marva went back into her own home and continued preparing for the day.

When Charlee returned, she came with her mother, a prepaid cell phone her father had purchased for Charlee and Zach to use in emergencies, a Disney World water bottle, a stuffed monkey, and the brightest, broadest smile Marva had ever seen on either a child or primate.

"You must be Charlee's mother," Marva said at the front door. "My name is Marva Ferguson."

"Yes, hello. I'm Emily. Emily Alexander." They shook hands across the threshold, while Charlee ducked underneath their arms and slithered into the house.

"Charlee!" her mother said.

"It's all right—come on in."

"I can't, actually, I'm late for work. I just wanted to be sure this was okay. Charlee helping you, I mean."

"Of course, yes. I'd love the company for as long as she'd like to stay. We've got a lot in store." Marva swept her arm behind her into her home like a game show host revealing the grand prize.

"You're sure?"

"I'm sure."

"She has a phone she can use to call me or her father—he's at work, too. Her brother, Zach, is home if she needs anything."

"Understood, but we'll be fine."

Emily smiled, and Marva could see both belief and relief on her face. Then Emily shouted a quick good-bye to Charlee, looked at her watch, and thanked Marva for keeping her daughter busy. Then she raced back across the field to the family van.

Marva closed the door with a smile.

7

The Advent Calendar

W here do we start?" Charlee asked.

"How about a tour?"

Miss Marva led Charlee around the home, and her eyes grew wider with each new room. It wasn't a large home, but to Charlee's Hershey's Kiss-colored eyes at less than five feet from the floor, it was a mansion. Charlee couldn't tell if it was bigger than the home they'd left behind, but they'd been vacuum-packed in the trailer long enough that Miss Marva's home felt bigger than the mall they used to visit on weekends.

They continued through every room, even Miss Marva's bedroom because Charlee asked, and Charlee gawked at every apron, figurine, book, and lamp as if they belonged to royalty.

"This is a palace, Miss Marva!"

"You're very sweet, Charlee, but it's just a house. Just my little home."

Miss Marva stopped at a bookcase in the living room. "Want to see one of my most favorite collections?"

"More favorite than the aprons?"

"It's close." Miss Marva winked and gestured grandly at three shelves full of books.

"What are they?"

"They're Bibles. I have them from all over the world in all different languages."

"Coooool," Charlee said. "Have you read them all?"

"No." She smiled. "But I've read this one many times." She tapped the spine of a brown leather Bible.

"Can I read it, too?"

"My Bibles are your Bibles, Charlee. . . . But first, speaking of aprons, follow me." Miss Marva led her into the pantry. "Everyone who decorates has to wear an apron." She reached for a peg of aprons and separated a few so the fronts could be read.

"Really?"

"Pick one."

"To wear?"

"My. Well, of course to wear. Are you here to work?"

"Yes, ma'am."

"Then pick an apron and let's get started."

Charlee spent so long considering her choices that Miss Marva excused herself for a visit to the restroom. When she returned, Charlee had on an apron that looked more like a dress.

On it, a woman held a candy bar in one hand and a box of chocolates in the other. The front read *I have this theory that chocolate slows down the aging process. It may not be true, but do I dare take the chance?*

Miss Marva smiled at Charlee. "Nice choice."

"I mostly liked the picture," Charlee said, holding out the apron skirt to admire it again.

Miss Marva tied a knot in the neck strap to make it smaller, and when she let it hang again, the apron's hem stopped at Charlee's ankles.

"How do I look?" she asked, taking a spin and letting the apron flare.

"It's perfect," Miss Marva said. "Let's get started."

Charlee and Miss Marva spent the morning arranging many of the decorations on the kitchen and dining room tables and taking a dust rag to those needing the care. They tested strings of lights and were pleased to find all of them illuminated when plugged in.

"That's never happened before," Miss Marva said. "You must be good luck, Charlee."

The words made Charlee illuminate, too.

They popped popcorn to freshen the decorative strings Miss Marva had been using for more Christmases than Charlee had been alive, and Miss Marva took the opportunity to explain why she never believed in throwing decorations away.

"Every year I just keep adding. One year I imagine my tree won't hold the weight anymore."

The idea made Charlee laugh, and she stood with her arms extended like tree branches and Miss Marva strung tinsel around her until Charlee pretended to topple to the floor from the weight.

At noon they broke for lunch—half a ham sandwich, extra popcorn, and a glass of lemonade—and Charlee asked about a photo of two men on the wall. "You have a lot of photos of the man on the left, but not of the other one," she said.

"My. So perceptive, aren't we? You're right. The man on the left was—is—my husband, John. The young man on the right, in the uniform, is my son, J.R."

"The one you told me about."

"The one who passed away, yes, that's right."

"Did he die in a war?"

"Unfortunately, yes. J.R. died in the Vietnam War. I bet you'll learn about that some day."

"I hope not," Charlee said.

Miss Marva took a drink of lemonade and delicately wiped her mouth.

"Why do you call him J.R.?"

"His name was really John Jr., after his father, but we called him Junior when he was a little boy. Then when he grew up, he liked J.R. better."

"I like J.R. better, too," Charlee said, and Miss Marva smiled her approval.

They finished lunch quickly, and Charlee was happy to get back to work. She told Miss Marva over and over that she'd never put up so many Christmas decorations in her whole life, and that each new item was cuter than the last. She especially enjoyed adding decorations to the tree and confessed that they might not have one of their own.

"No tree?"

"I don't think so. I don't know really, I guess. But I don't think so."

"My. Well, you can come see my tree anytime. All right? My tree is your tree this year."

They passed from room to room, not moving on until each one could be mistaken for Santa's home. When they both began to tire, they stopped to sit on the couch and look at photos or share a funny Christmas story from their past. Charlee revealed Melvin the monkey's history and bragged about her father. "He's an amazing monkey storyteller."

"Your dad's a monkey?" Miss Marva asked and Charlee snickered.

Next they sat side-by-side on the couch and dusted each piece of the nativity, even though Charlee couldn't see a speck of dirt. "Are you sure these are dirty?" she asked.

"Even the dust you can't see needs to be wiped away, right?"

"Right!" Charlee said with a big nod, even though she didn't really understand. She watched Miss Marva pass a cloth through every crease of each nativity piece, and she mimicked her every move like an apprentice shadowing the master.

They placed the pieces one at a time on the coffee table in the middle of the living room. They started with Joseph, then Mary, the three kings, a shepherd, a standing angel, an ox, a donkey, and a camel. Charlee watched Miss Marva rearrange the pieces with such care, she almost wondered if her best friend had been there that night. The final piece was the infant Jesus. But after it was placed, Miss Marva picked it right back up again and polished the smooth stone figurine in her hand. When she was done, she held it another moment before returning the Savior to Mary's feet.

"Are you crying, Miss Marva?"

"No, dear, just praying."

"With tears?"

Miss Marva used the tail of her apron to dab her eyes dry. "Sometimes crying and praying are the same thing." She smiled the words.

It wasn't long until it was time to finish the day with one final project.

"I should have asked you this before, Charlee, because this is very important."

Charlee's eyebrows rose, and she stiffened her spine.

"Do you have any experience with Advent calendars?"

"A little."

"How much?"

"We used to have one."

"Perfect!" Miss Marva grabbed her by the hand and led her back to the mantel in the living room. "Wait here."

A moment later she returned from the kitchen carrying the wooden box. She set it on the edge of the coffee table next to the nativity scene. "This is my favorite part of Christmas. It's the very best part of the holiday."

"Better than the tree?" Charlee asked, her mouth gaping in disbelief.

"Much," Miss Marva said, then she took a rolled-up piece of white cotton fabric from the box and rolled it out across the mantel. Charlee noticed that it fit perfectly and thought it a miracle her friend had found a piece exactly the right size.

Miss Marva pulled out the wooden Advent calendar from the box and held it so Charlee could admire it up close. It was mostly Christmas red with gold, hand-painted lettering. Charlee counted twenty-six numbered doors to open, and each one had a matching golden star attached as a small knob.

Charlee let a peaceful moment pass, the kind she felt after she said amen to her daily and nightly prayers. Then she asked, "Miss Marva, why are there twenty-six days on your Advent calendar? Isn't Christmas always on December 25th?"

Miss Marva's tired laugh was cut short by the doorbell ringing and the sight of Charlee's brother, Zach, standing on the porch.

When Charlee pulled open the door, Zach pointed with his thumb toward their trailer. "Time to go home."

Charlee frowned. "Okay, but you have to meet Miss Marva first."

Miss Marva looked him over from head to toe and smiled at him. "I bet I could guess who this is."

"Really?" Charlee said.

Miss Marva extended her hand. "You must be Zach."

"Hey," he answered. He shook her hand, but when it appeared he was trying to let go, Marva grabbed it with her other hand, too.

"I knew it was you because Charlee told me how handsome you were."

"Really?" Charlee said again.

"You did, and you told me he's the best big brother you could ever have."

"He's the only brother I have," Charlee said, looking up at Miss Marva.

"And aren't you so lucky," Miss Marva said, and she finally let go of Zach's hand.

Charlee looked at her brother. She knew him well enough to know he was trying not to smile. Her mother had told her teenage boys were good at that.

"Nice to meet you, too," Zach said. "Time to go home, Charlee."

Charlee hugged Miss Marva good-bye and thought it was strange that when they got halfway across the field, Zach looked back over his shoulder without breaking stride. Charlee did the same and then smiled.

Miss Marva was still watching them.

8
Emily's Journal

It's Thursday, November 17. This is my first entry in the new journal. I can't believe I've already filled one up this year. Usually one lasts me through December, and I still have blank pages left at the end.

I dug up my old journal box this morning to put the last one in it. I thought about reading some of the entries from earlier this year, but I'm afraid it will only made me feel sad, and I'm trying not to be sad.

So maybe one day. And maybe one day, they'll all be interesting to the kids. For now I don't think I can handle reminders of the old life and how much better it was than this new one. I'm just hanging on and that's got to be all right for now.

Thanksgiving is one week away. But we will not be eating here in the trailer. (I still refuse to call it a home because I am afraid that if I do it will become permanent.) Charlee's best friend in the world is a woman from the neighborhood. Her name is Marva Ferguson; Charlee calls her "Miss Marva." She lives in a nice home at the edge of the trailer park. She's been here for a long time. She owned all this land around us once. She and her husband, that is. They sold it and were able to keep the area where her home sits.

We are eating Thanksgiving dinner in her home. It's an odd thing, I think. But Charlee cried when we first said no. She said she wasn't upset that we were not eating there, she was upset that the rest of us didn't want to get to know her "best friend forever."

So Thomas and I went over and spent time with Miss Marva that night, and we accepted her invitation. We offered to bring something, but she insisted that we simply come early. She wants me to wear one of her aprons and help her. I did not tell Thomas this, or Marva, but a part of me is looking forward to it. Even though my pride hates the idea that I cannot afford a traditional meal in my own ~~home~~ trailer.

Miss Marva and Charlee spend time together after school every day, and it is a gift to us. She has always been an "old soul," but I have not understood what that meant until now. She relates so well with adults. She always has. Maybe no one should be surprised that she is friends with a woman who is at least eighty years old.

Sometimes I watch the two of them working slowly at Marva's clothesline and I wish I were there too. One day maybe I'll surprise them and walk over early before I call her home for dinner.

I am very proud that Charlee has survived this change to

our life and to our family so well. Better than Zach. Better than Thomas or me.

Thomas . . . Thomas continues to work every job he can. Lately he's been framing houses in a subdivision not far from here. I wish he would frame a home for us.

But he's better I think. As Thanksgiving and Christmas come closer, he seems to be getting happier. Tired but happier. We're not the couple we were before we got caught up in all this. All the life and the fights. But we're still here under the same roof every night, and I think that means something.

It's a good sign, I think, that Thomas is telling Charlee stories again and that he is rebuilding a 1967 VW Beetle with Zach that they got at the junkyard in exchange for fixing the roof on the owner's home. They're working on the ugly thing in the yard, even though Zach cannot drive until next summer.

If he lives that long.

Zach is still Zach. He still mopes like it's a sport he's lettering in. He's doing better in school, we think; his grades are still not very good, but they're better, and the phone hasn't rung yet. I have even caught him doing homework a few times. He told me the other day it will be a miracle if he graduates high school and he might end up washing plastic trays at the food court forever. I told him that if he did the work honestly and lived up to his honor and started to love his family again, I would visit him at the food court every day. I love that kid.

I am working at Walmart. It's a twenty-minute drive, but the pay is better than at the mini-mart in Woodbrook, and I get to meet so many interesting people. I've made friends and working there feels like our old life in small ways. No one really knows our story, and no one cares. No one judges or grills me about my life. I can just work with some of the nicest people I've ever known. I guess it's my escape from everything I see around me.

If only one thing matters, I guess it would be this. If my family ever reads this, please understand that I'm trying. I think we're all trying. We want to turn the corner and keep trying. And if we keep at it, I think we'll be fine. Yes. We'll be fine. Saying that makes me believe it more.

If we can live through this, we can live through anything.

9

Rusty Apronisms

$\mathbf{M}$arva had never spent so much money at the grocery store. Not when John was alive, and not even when J.R. was in high school and eating everything not nailed down. But she didn't mind; she knew the big tab meant a full house on Thanksgiving.

A snarky young man at the store had helped stuff grocery bags into every inch of her toy-sized Miata. With every new bag, he guaranteed her it wouldn't fit and that she'd be making two trips home and back again. But Marva simply smiled and thought that the bold youngster didn't know her very well.

By the time they finished their grocery Jenga, bags were arranged on the floor up front and puzzle-pieced into the trunk like clothes in a too-small suitcase. The turkey, a giant nineteen-pound bully, sat triple-bagged and buckled in the passenger's seat. Marva said a prayer on the drive home that someone in the neighborhood would be out and about and willing to help her carry in the load.

Marva drove slowly through 27 Homes but didn't see a single person outside until she hit the bend in the fishing hook. She rolled down her window and greeted the porch wavers, but she knew they couldn't help. She doubted they could carry a box of breadcrumbs if they had to.

She rounded the corner, rolled down the short straightaway, and pulled into her driveway.

"Thank you, God. I knew you were listening," Marva said when she saw her friend Rusty Cleveland leaning against his pickup truck.

"How's my favorite columnist?" Marva said, climbing from the car.

"I'm good. How are you?"

"Better, because you're here," she said, hugging him. "Would you give me a hand with a few groceries?"

Rusty reached for his back and feigned pain, but Marva threatened to sock him with a bag of frozen vegetables.

He agreed to help on the condition Marva watch from the porch.

She did not argue.

After three trips and a bad joke about Marva's turkey needing to hire a personal trainer, Rusty ran to his own vehicle and retrieved something for Marva. After helping put away the perishables, Rusty sat in the living room, and Marva sank into her chair.

"You look good," Rusty said.

"There you go, just like the mainstream media to twist the truth." She laughed at her own joke.

"But you do—you look very good, in fact."

"My. Well, you're a kind man, Rusty. A fibber, but a kind one, at least. I'm exhausted, and I haven't even cooked anything yet."

"Guests for Thanksgiving?" Rusty asked.

"Well, you didn't think I was going to eat all that, did you?"

Rusty smiled. "Who am I to judge?"

Marva looked at him and smiled back. She'd missed her friend's visits and took a minute to consider the last time he'd checked on her. "Yes," she finally said after a lengthy pause, "I am having guests this year. Some neighbors, the ones right across the field. I've become quite close."

"That's great."

"They're a young family. Young to me, anyway. Two children. The little one is a girl I just adore. She calls me her BBF."

"BFF, maybe?"

"That sounds right," Marva said. "They've had a hard go of it lately, and I don't guess they would have had much of a holiday."

"So here comes Miss Marva, just like always."

"Nothing anyone else wouldn't do."

"We both know that's not true, don't we?" Rusty reached into a bag that read Sabrina's Gifts and pulled out an apron.

Marva giggled at the price tag that still hung from it.

"You didn't see that," Rusty said.

"See what?"

Rusty stood and approached Marva's chair. "Don't get up. This is for you. I picked it up last month. No, back in September, I guess. It had your name on it." He held it up for Marva to read. The front of it had a large peanut with a mouth.

Marva read aloud. "You're a nut. (But not the tasty kind—you're more like the ones that make me swell up and require immediate medical attention.)"

She began cackling before she'd even finished. "That's one of my favorite apronisms ever."

"You like it?"

"I love it." Marva pushed herself up and hugged him. "Thank you for thinking of me. Even if I am a nut."

Marva escorted him to the porch with her arm looped through his, and they shared a few more minutes of small talk about laundry, some of Marva's other new aprons, Woodbrook politics, Charlee, the newspaper, Marva's volunteer schedule, and Rusty's family.

"Thank you for the visit," Marva said. "It means so much. You know that, right?"

"I do."

"So you'll be back?"

"I will."

10
Thanksgiving Day

Charlee woke with an upset stomach that choked her appetite for off-brand Cookie Crisp, but it did not slow her excitement for the holiday. It was going to be the Alexander family's most exciting day since moving to Woodbrook two months earlier. Her dad was off for two days. Her mother had to work Black Friday at Walmart, but at least she could spend Thanksgiving at home.

Charlee sat at the chipped laminate kitchen table across from her mother and made a list on a free notepad from Woodbrook Credit Union.

Take a shower
Let Mom curl my hair
Make place setting cards
Leave for Miss Marva's at 11 sharp

Give a tour
Help make dinner
Eat dinner
Eat dessert!
Clean up
Make Zach help
Watch movie as a family!
Walk home

They hadn't seen a movie together since long before arriving at 27 Homes, and Miss Marva had invited them to stay after the feast to watch something on the fancy television she hardly used. Zach wasn't convinced, but Charlee was sure that by the time dinner was done, he would love Miss Marva just like she did, and he wouldn't ever want to go home.

"That's quite a list," Charlee's mother said.

"I know! There's more probably, but these are the big things."

Emily pushed herself away from the table. "How about some toast and a glass of milk? Does that sound good?"

But Charlee didn't hear her; she was adding stars to her favorite items on the day's to-do list.

"How about an apple?" Emily asked, her head in the refrigerator. "It's a little ripe, but it's still good."

Charlee didn't hear that, either. She was drawing a stick figure wearing an apron to the right of Miss Marva's name. Of course, the apron was much bigger than her body, and Charlee added a heart in the middle of it.

"How about my famous, hot and juicy, fish guts casserole, Charlee? I have one of those in the oven. Does that sound better?"

But the suggestion didn't reel Charlee in from her daydream about an afternoon with all the people she loved most all in one place.

Emily soon placed two pieces of toast in front of Charlee and slid the notepad away from her to the other side of the table. "Eat something, please."

In the yard, Zach and his dad were already working on the dusty, rusty Beetle that was taking so long to come back to life; Charlee had suggested there would be flying cars before theirs ever ran again. Watching them through the window, she admitted to her mother that she worried her dad and Zach might spend the whole day covered in grease, listening to loud music, and forget to come to Miss Marva's for Thanksgiving.

Emily assured her daughter with a kiss on the head that the Alexander men would not miss the big day for anything. "They'll be there."

After breakfast, Charlee showered and enjoyed having her hair blow-dried by her mother. It wasn't as long as she wanted it yet, but it was long enough to curl, and Miss Marva had said that if her best friend would curl her hair, she'd curl hers, too.

Dressed and ready to go long before anyone else, Charlee sat back at the kitchen table and made place cards for everyone using half sheets of cardstock and crayons. Each card had the first and last name of the guest. First names were in red; last names were in green. She even made one for Melvin and gave him the middle name Mason, just for fun.

"Melvin Mason Alexander. It sounds like a president's name," she told the stuffed monkey with the big teeth.

With the cards done and time left to kill, Charlee lay on the bottom bunk in the room she shared with Zach and rested her head on her hand, careful not to unfurl her shiny black curls. To keep her dress from wrinkling, she pulled the edges straight. It was the only nice dress she'd saved from the moving sale, and it was orange with oversized, white polka dots. When Charlee got tired at night, she thought the dots looked like the moon. A hazy, off-white band encircled each dot, and she counted them as she lay in bed.

She could tell her hair smelled delicious, and she couldn't resist the urge to pull a curl toward her nose and enjoy the scent of her mother's shampoo. The aroma made her feel like a grown-up, and Charlee couldn't wait to share the new smell and the new look with Miss Marva.

She tried to read a book she got from the library, but the excitement of the day made it hard to focus. So she gave in and lay flat, gazing up at the bottom of Zach's bed and wishing the clock wasn't stuck on boring.

Charlee looked at the sunflower clock on the wall. "It's eleven!" she shouted at 10:58.

"I'll be right there," her mother called from her bedroom at the rear of the trailer.

"All right, I'll walk slow," Charlee said, stepping outside and beginning the journey. She stopped at the fallen fence that separated their yard from the communal field and turned back to see her mother whisper something in her father's ear. Then she waited impatiently for her mother to catch up.

Heavy rain and unseasonably warm temperatures had turned the grass in the field green and sent it high into the late-November air. Mother and daughter weaved through the field, giggling and pointing and sidestepping small puddles like unafraid soldiers in a foreign minefield.

When they arrived at the stone pathway just before the clothesline, they found Miss Marva waiting on the porch. Her silver hair was lightly curled, and the style revealed how thin her hair was.

"You did it! Your hair looks so nice!" Charlee said.

Miss Marva smiled and fluffed it with both hands. "You're kind, but yours looks truly beautiful. You look like a glamorous supermodel. But prettier."

Charlee looked up at her mother, and Emily winked in agreement.

"So how do you like my apron?" Miss Marva asked. It was white and featured extra-thick gold stitching and a photo of a sweet potato. Above the picture appeared the question *Thankful for You?* Then below the image, it read *Yes, I Yam.*

Miss Marva motioned for Emily to step closer. "All right,

dear Emily, I do hate to hide that lovely blouse, but an apron is required to complete the outfit." She held one up for her to admire. It was dark green and featured a large pumpkin pie divided into slices—with two pieces clearly missing. Above the pie, in white block print, it read *Happy Thanksgiving! Take two and call me in the morning.*

Emily slipped it on and promised to eat at least two pieces of pie before the end of the day.

Then Miss Marva pulled open Charlee's apron so she could read it more easily. Charlee immediately noticed that the bottom had been trimmed; it was much shorter than the other aprons she'd seen before. It was cream-colored and the loopy, cursive text was dandelion yellow. It read *Charlee Alexander.*

Charlee had both hands over her mouth as Miss Marva draped the custom-sized apron around her neck.

"Why don't you?" she said to Emily, and Miss Marva stepped aside so Charlee's mother could tie the apron around her daughter's waist.

When it was tied in the perfect bow, Emily spun Charlee back around and said, "It's beautiful," but quickly corrected herself. "No, *you're* beautiful."

Miss Marva walked toward her front door and, without looking back, raised her right arm and announced, "Let's cook!"

Charlee gave her mother the promised tour while Miss Marva finished preparing supplies and ingredients in the kitchen. Charlee pointed out every photo, every Christmas decoration, and every piece of interesting history. She described the wooden Advent calendar in great detail, as if her mother weren't standing right next to her. Then she suggested her mother shouldn't touch it. "It's very delicate, Mom."

After the tour, Charlee asked permission to put the place cards on the dining room table, even though it wasn't set yet, and she was thrilled that Miss Marva said she could decide who sat where. Charlee arranged the seats, then rearranged them, then asked her mother's opinion, and switched them one more time. She'd run around the table so much she was dizzy when she finally settled on the assignments.

The three chefs held what Miss Marva called a turkey talk session in the kitchen to plan the day. The turkey was already in the oven, but that was the easy part, Miss Marva said. And before Charlee knew the meeting was even over, the kitchen burst alive with breadcrumbs and flour flying, mixers mixing, and pie tins rattling. Charlee had never seen hands move so quickly through the air.

She also hadn't seen her mother smile and laugh so much since the move to Woodbrook.

As the morning turned to afternoon, the three friends broke for a snack and to taste Miss Marva's Thanksgiving cider. They sat in the living room and played a game to identify the scents that filled the house. Each time one of them closed her eyes and concentrated, she smelled something different.

"There's the stuffing," Miss Marva said.

Charlee went next. "I smell pecan pie."

"Mmm, cranberry sauce," Emily said, her eyes still closed.

The game continued until Charlee began naming things they hadn't even prepared yet. The women laughed and soaked in the company until the afternoon demanded they get back to work. When Miss Marva and Emily returned to the kitchen, Charlee leaned back into the soft couch and put her hands behind her head. She looked up at a ceiling fan and dreamed about a life where days like today spun around and around, repeating themselves perfectly until someone turned off the switch for just a few minutes.

The doorbell startled her, and when she sat up, she realized she'd napped for an hour and her father and brother were standing at the front door. She pulled it open and asked, "Want a tour?"

Miss Marva stood at the head of the table at 5:00 P.M. and welcomed everyone to her home. Charlee found that odd since she and her mother had been there most of the day, but she smiled and said "Thank you" anyway.

Charlee's dad sat on the opposite end of the table from Miss Marva with Zach on one side and Emily on the other. Charlee sat by her mother and, across from her, Melvin the monkey sat on two stacked throw pillows from the couch.

Charlee thought the table looked like a scene from a television commercial. A giant turkey sat on the table in front of her father. Stuffing surrounded it on the china platter like clouds. Her mother had made Waldorf salad, which Charlee didn't like but would eat anyway because she could pick out the apples. There were hot rolls made from scratch and real butter—not the waxy spread that tasted like the plastic tub it came in.

Her mouth watered at the heaping mountain of mashed potatoes. Steam rose from them, and Charlee admired the melting hunk of butter she'd placed so perfectly at the tip-top.

The table also held yams with marshmallows, corn on the cob, green beans, two kinds of squash, and another vegetable she'd never seen before. Right in front of Melvin sat a plate of deviled eggs; Charlee would eat one of those first, by tradition. Tradition also demanded that Charlee not leave the table until she'd placed a black olive on each of her fingertips. Zach used to do it, too, but she thought he was probably too old for that.

"Let us pray," Miss Marva said, and even Melvin bowed his head with an assist.

"Dear Father, we gather on this Thanksgiving Day so grateful for so many blessings. But mostly, Father, we are grateful for the gift of friendship. We thank thee for bringing Charlee and her family into my home this day. May they be blessed with all that they need, Father. We ask also that Thou would bless our troops, wherever they might be, and bless the leaders of our country, that they would turn to Thee, and also please bless all the pastors and preachers of the world, whatever church they might belong to. Finally, dear Father, we are thankful for this food and ask that Thou would bless it. May we be strong, happy, and healthy. In Jesus' name, amen."

They each added an "Amen!"—Charlee's was the loudest—and they began to fill their plates. Charlee's parents took turns saying things like, "This is so much food. You're so kind to do this. Are you sure we can't contribute toward the cost? This turkey must have been expensive. It all smells so delicious, Marva, thank you."

They only stopped when Marva playfully threatened to not share any pie if they didn't simply enjoy the meal and their time together.

While Charlee ate slowly and enjoyed every bite like it was her last, Zach sat across the table and took bites so big Charlee told him he could have swallowed the turkey whole. When Emily asked him to slow down, Zach stuffed half a roll in his mouth and apologized at the same time.

"You're so gross," Charlee said.

"It's all right," Miss Marva said. "He's just hungry, right, Zach?" While he nodded a yes, Miss Marva took the biggest bite of stuffing Charlee had ever seen. It was so big, a chunk fell off her heaping fork when she put it in her mouth.

When everyone but Zach began filling their plates for seconds—Zach was going for thirds—Miss Marva slapped the table next to her plate. "My! Oh my, I nearly forgot the gumdrops with all the excitement."

"Gumdrops?" Charlee's voice rose.

"Yes, I put a bowl out every year. They were my son's favorite. J.R. always had to have a bowl on the table when he was young, and it became a tradition in our family. It was our little reminder that Christmas was right around the corner, and that while we loved Thanksgiving, the most important holiday would arrive before we knew it."

"That's sweet," Emily said.

"I'll get them for you," Charlee offered, jumping up from her chair.

"Wonderful, dear. I've already got them in a glass candy dish on the kitchen counter, right next to the microwave. Thank you."

Charlee dashed from the room and heard the adults behind her laugh as she skipped down the hallway. She pushed open the swinging kitchen door, and her eyes found the dish on the counter. Charlee picked it up and spun back around on her feet, but when she stopped spinning, the room didn't.

She tumbled forward and heard the sound of her head hitting the square kitchen table.

The bowl fell from her hands, and the thin glass shattered on the floor into more pieces than there were gumdrops.

Removed from the pain, Charlee thought she heard her body hit the floor in stages: first her hips, then her legs, chest, arms, and head. It sounded like an old woman's slow clap.

Four sets of heavy feet clopped down the hallway, but Charlee did not hear those sounds.

She did not hear the sound of hinges squeaking on the kitchen door.

She did not hear the door slam with violence against the inside wall.

She did not hear the scream of her mother.

11
Black Friday

Marva stood up for the fourth time to stretch her legs.

The stiff, cool, green plastic seat didn't invite anyone to sit for long. Instead, it seemed to suggest that weary emergency room visitors would be better off if they went home and sat in their own soft, warm, living room chairs to await the news.

Marva stood again at the bank of vending machines and examined the selection of stale Honey Buns and generic corn chips as if they'd somehow changed in the last hour, or the hour before, or the one before that.

She stretched her back and felt the pain of eight decades collecting and collapsing on her spine. She'd been remarkably healthy her entire life, having spent much more time in hospitals in behalf of John's health and other loved ones than for her own issues. But spending Thanksgiving Day on her feet and moving around the kitchen with the energy of a celebrity chef had taken its toll.

Tired as she was, Marva's emotions were even more battered. She examined her face in the reflection of the vending machine and put her hands on her cheeks. Her eyes were heavy and sore. She'd cried in the car all the way to Woodbrook Mercy Hospital, following the ambulance close enough that she could see paramedics buzzing above Charlee through the small rear window.

Reflected behind her, she could see Charlee's family spread out across a row of seats across the waiting room. Charlee's mother had ridden in the front of the ambulance, and Thomas had sprinted to the house to get Emily's purse and the family minivan.

All the frantic motion had left Zach at Marva's, and he stood on the porch watching the ambulance lights bounce off the trailers of 27 Homes as it navigated down the fishhook and onto the main highway.

"What are we waiting for?" Marva had said, bursting from the house with her coat and car keys. "Let's go." While she drove and began to cry, Zach popped his knuckles in the passenger's seat.

"Is she going to be okay?" Zach had asked.

"I don't know, Zach. I don't know."

"Did she trip?"

"I didn't see. I wish I had."

"Was she sleeping on the floor? It looked like she was sleeping."

"I don't know, son, I just don't know."

Marva turned away from the snack machine and watched the family of three sitting like lonely islands in the green sea of seats. Zach clutched his knees, his sneakers pulled up onto the chair. Thomas sat with his legs extended and his head back, his eyes pointed to the ceiling or heaven, Marva couldn't tell which. Emily sat with her legs crossed over one another and her arms folded tightly across her chest in a hug that she must have wished came from someone else.

Since arriving at the ER, they'd watched the room fill and empty around them. They'd seen a broken arm from a backyard Turkey Bowl football game, minor burns from a deep fryer, two people with flu-like symptoms, and a baby whose cries could still be heard from behind the double doors that separated the ill from the healthy like an iron curtain.

Charlee's mother and father had taken turns at her unconscious side back in the belly of the hospital, but eventually had both been asked to sit outside while the doctors awaited the results from the latest test—an MRI. They'd taken Charlee's blood, hooked her up to heart and breathing monitors, and promised an update before midnight.

Marva made a loop around the waiting room and smiled again at the nurse at the triage desk. She paused to put her hand on Emily's shoulder for a moment before slowly looping once more. When she returned again to Emily's seat, she took the one next to her and looked at the clock on the wall near the mounted television. She compared the time to her watch and realized that, without fanfare, the day had turned from Thanksgiving to Black Friday.

At 12:30 A.M., two doctors appeared through the emergency room doors and surveyed the scene. Only Marva and the Alexander family remained. One of the doctors was familiar from earlier in the night, but the other was a stranger, and he introduced himself as a neurologist.

"Would you like to find someplace more private?" he asked.

"No," Emily said, standing and speaking for the family. "How is she?"

Both Thomas and Zach stood, too.

The neurologist motioned for them to retake their seats, and he crouched down in front of them. The other doctor stood behind him, clutching a clipboard. Marva thought he wore the kind of stoic look of a man working much too hard to hide bad news. Still standing nearby, she decided to ease out of the private conversation but remained close enough to capture the essentials.

"We've reviewed the MRI and CT scan," the neurologist said, looking at Emily. "It's serious."

"From hitting her head?"

"No." His eyes moved to Thomas. "Mr. and Mrs. Alexander. It's a tumor."

Emily gasped, and the doctor placed his hand on her knee. "What?" Thomas asked.

"Your daughter has a brain tumor."

Thomas stood, and the neurologist followed to his feet.

Marva took Thomas's seat at Emily's side and put her arm around her shoulders.

"A brain tumor?" Thomas repeated, and Marva found the words even more sharp the second time she heard them.

"We've got another neurologist on the way here, a colleague, but yes, it's quite clear on the scans." He paused and took a long breath. "We're not wasting a minute, Mr. and Mrs. Alexander."

Emily dropped her head in her hands.

"So what? You operate? You can take it out, right? You'll just take it out?" Thomas demanded.

"Yes, the first step will be surgery, and a neurosurgeon has been called. The surgery will almost certainly happen today. But if it's what we think, it will take more."

"More surgery?"

"More treatment. I don't want to get in front of the other doctors here—we have a lot of information to gather—but I think we're going to have to be aggressive in this case."

"Aggressive?" Thomas said sharply, and Emily finally sat up and steadied herself on her armrests.

"It looks like a PNET—a primitive neuroectodermal

tumor. It's near the back of her brain. We call it a medullo-blastoma. I know that doesn't mean anything to you yet. It shouldn't. But you should know that this could be a fast-growing, possibly malignant, tumor."

"Cancer," Emily whispered.

"We'll know more after the surgery, of course. But we suspect it will take radiation and chemotherapy to control it."

Thomas looked away from the neurologist and to the other doctor. "This is a mistake—a mistake. She was fine today. She cooked dinner. She and Marva—they worked all the day on it. Didn't they, Emily? Didn't you, Marva? You worked all day on Thanksgiving. Charlee helped and laughed. Then she went for gumdrops." He looked at his wife. "She just went for gum-drops, Emily. Gumdrops."

Marva watched the doctors exchange a glance before the neurologist said, "We'll know more soon. I'm sure it feels like this news is coming from nowhere, but the truth is, this illness has probably been coming for a while. Who knows how long the tumor has been there, but we're lucky to have caught it now, while we have options and a chance to form a plan."

"Options," Emily said, staring at the doctors.

"I understand—*we understand*—this is a shock. But we're going to be aggressive in our treatment and do all we can as quickly as we can. We know a lot about these tumors, and Charlee is not alone. This is the most common of childhood brain tumors."

Emily stood and crossed her arms again. "She's not going to die, right?"

"Of course not," Thomas answered. "No."

The first doctor spoke up. "Children beat this all the time."

"All the time?" Emily asked.

The neurologist hesitated before putting a hand on her arm. "We're going to do everything we can with the best people around us. Charlee is still asleep, but we'll come get you when she wakes, and, hopefully, by then we'll know more. We'll have the entire team here, and we can get started immediately."

At 11:35 A.M., Charlee was rolled into surgery while Marva, Zach, Emily, and Thomas sat in a more comfortable and private waiting room.

Marva returned to 27 Homes with a key to the Alexanders' trailer and a list. Thomas asked if she'd mind collecting a change of clothes for each of them, Zach's iPod and backpack, a file folder with the family's expired health insurance information, Thomas's cell phone charger, and Melvin the monkey.

She also spent an hour in her own home changing her clothes and cleaning up the crusty, sour remnants of Thanksgiving. The dinner table looked like a wonderful dream that had ended too early with the jolt of an unfriendly alarm clock. Charlee's fork still sat on her plate, jousting a piece of white turkey she'd dipped in the potato and gravy swimming pool.

She rinsed but did not wash the dishes. She had swept up the strange mix of shattered glass and gumdrops before she realized she had not bothered to put on an apron. She promised herself she would share that odd fact with Charlee when she saw her again and prayed that Charlee would playfully scold her.

On the way back to the hospital, she stopped and bought $30 worth of sandwiches in the hope she'd bring something the family would enjoy. She was grateful that Zach and Thomas both found something they liked and was very satisfied that they'd finally eaten something. After some coaxing from Marva, and despite assurances of not being hungry, Emily finally chose and dressed a club sandwich. But then she averted her eyes from it, like it was a stranger she did not want to talk to.

Marva gave in and let Emily be; she was out of energy for anything else. She could not remember when her bones had been more tired. All that was left in her was to sit and watch each of the Alexanders process the shock of the day.

Emily's attention went from a window overlooking the parking garage to a muted television running a syndicated talk show Marva did not recognize.

Thomas texted someone on his cell phone, and it dinged almost constantly with replies.

Zach sat in the only chair in the room that reclined, listening to music. Marva would have thought he was asleep, except that his hands occasionally rose above his chest and he looked to be playing the air drums.

Marva gathered all the images together and wished she knew precisely what they thought and how she could help. She considered whether she belonged there at all, if she was intruding, whether they knew she was even there anymore and if she should wait at home.

Marva also considered whether Charlee would ever hang laundry with her again. Would she wear one of Marva's aprons? Pick dandelions? Spin on the stump?

She had a hundred questions and only exhausted guesses for answers. When all the questions came and went, when the answers tumbled into one sad unknown, Marva was left with only one: Would Charlee live to see Christmas?

12
Balloons

Charlee looked at the bouquet of yellow balloons in her room and didn't have to see the card to know they were from her best friend. Miss Marva had sent other balloons too, and flowers, and candy which she could only eat a tiny piece at a time.

The room reminded her of family birthdays, and she stared at the balloons and remembered the days when birthdays were a grand production. Once upon a time, they'd been better than her favorite movies, the kind they stood in line for. They were way better than that unbearably long musical they saw in Washington, DC, during their old life in their old town on Eyring Avenue.

Birthdays for the Alexanders weren't just a party after dinner, or a trip to Gabby's—their favorite pizza place. Charlee's mother and father said they hadn't had many nice birthdays when they were kids, so they'd promised that Charlee and Zach would have what they didn't.

Birthdays began in the morning with balloons, one for every year of the person's life, and whatever breakfast treat had been requested. One year, Zach had tacos for breakfast. Charlee once had gummy bear pancakes. Even their parents had special birthdays, and they always seemed to pick something for breakfast they knew the rest of the family would like, too.

The whole family also played a game that Charlee's mother said started when Zach was a baby. Only the first person to see the birthday boy or girl that morning was allowed to sing "Happy Birthday." Everyone else had to wait until the cake was served later that day. The best strategy was to be there when the birthday person walked sleepy-eyed out of his or her bedroom, or to wait just around the corner, or to stand just outside the bathroom door when they finally came out of a long shower. Zach said he was growing tired of it, but Charlee knew he still secretly liked all the fuss.

Birthday dinners were also up to the person celebrating. Sometimes they chose to go out, sometimes they ate at home, but no matter what, everyone was together and the balloons always made the trip. After dinner, but before the cake, everyone gathered in a circle and said something they had learned that year from the birthday boy, girl, mom, or dad. Usually the activity turned into a tickle fight or giggle contest, and everyone laughed until their stomachs hurt. Then they ate cake and ice cream until their stomachs hurt even worse.

Once, when Charlee's dad was traveling for work and staying in a hotel a day's drive away, he still came all the way home for dinner, cake, and presents. They didn't start until 11:00 P.M. and didn't get to bed until after 1:00 A.M. But it had been one of Charlee's favorite birthdays.

Charlee lay in her hospital bed and wondered how many balloons it would take to float out of Woodbrook Mercy Hospital and all the way home. It had been two weeks since Thanksgiving, two weeks since the surgery, two weeks since the last time her mother's eyes were clear. Now they were red and swollen and looked like they weighed so much it hurt to keep them open.

Charlee had already started chemotherapy and radiation. She'd heard the doctors say they didn't want to do them at the same time, but because of the kind of tumor they found, they didn't want to take any chances. She'd also heard them say it wouldn't be long before she started losing her hair, and that made her very unhappy. She tried to stay positive, the way her mother told her to. But she'd waited a long time for her long hair to come back, and, in Charlee's mind, losing it again was the most unfair thing of all.

Charlee thought about Miss Marva and wondered when she'd come back to visit. She hadn't been in for a few days, and Charlee worried about her. Miss Marva didn't have anyone to send her balloons when she didn't feel well or to sit by her bed when she was tired and wanted to hear a book.

Charlee looked at Melvin on her bedside table. He was the only one still smiling. She imagined the room full of balloons, a dozen white ones by the top of the bed, a dozen purple by her feet, a couple dozen more on the machine hooked to her arm, and a few on the tubes, too. She squinted her eyes and saw five bundles, maybe six or seven or eight, all tied to the couch where her mom slept. She figured if her dad were on it, too, it would need a bunch more to get it off the ground, so she pictured those, too.

She began to feel sleepy again and pulled Melvin close. The real balloons began to blend into the imaginary ones, and she felt herself being lifted from the bed. She clutched Melvin tight and smiled.

13

Missing Marva

6:17 A.M.

Marva awoke and looked at the clock the same way she always did. But she did not swing her legs toward the floor, turn off the alarm, and pick up the phone on the nightstand to check for a dial tone. Instead, she simply reached over and turned off the alarm.

When she tucked her arms back under the warm blanket, she felt just how much her sides ached. Then, as she readjusted the sheets, her legs sent the clear message they were not ready to support her and probably could not be counted on if she had elaborate plans for the day.

6:20.

It took just a few minutes for her to receive the same message from the rest of her body, too. There would be no working at the clothesline. She would not walk to the Alexanders to check on Zach and watch him play his video games or ask him about his day at school. She'd enjoyed those visits the last two weeks, and they'd taken her mind off her own aches and pains. But that morning, the years screamed louder than they ever had, certainly louder than the old alarm clock.

7:04.

Marva felt guilty. She'd never been a sleeper, even when she and John used to work late; they'd always arise on time and make up for their fatigue by going to bed early. She remembered teasing John about the times they had to shut all the blinds in the house and wear sleeping masks during the spring and summer in order to race the sun to sleep. She also remembered the early years of their marriage, when they went to bed early quite often, even when they weren't tired at all. The thought made her smile.

8:53.

Marva turned away from the clock and wished John was next to her. She thought of the mornings she first started checking for the dial tone. Those were the days after they stopped hearing from J.R. as he fought in Vietnam. It wasn't that he'd called every day, but rarely a week passed when they didn't hear his voice at least once on a scratchy line run between their home and a tent in Asia. He never wrote much, like other soldiers they knew in the war, but he called home more often than many. He said he liked the sound of their voices, the instant assurance that they were alive. Letters, he said, were outdated before they left the jungle.

10:33.

Marva was awake again and still thinking about J.R. She finally reached over and listened for the dial tone. Like every single day since the first time she'd checked, it was there.

Her stomach ached, and she didn't know whether she was hungry, sick, lonely, or some combination of everything, some sensation required by old age. She'd felt its cousin before, the kind of loneliness so deep it paralyzes. But the feelings of that particular morning were unfamiliar, a new neighbor she was inclined to distrust.

10:59.

There were no trailers in the neighborhood on the morning the Army chaplain turned down their driveway. There was only 1 Home, not 21 or 24 or 27. There weren't kids throwing rocks or cursing at their parents. There was just the Ferguson family with a nice yard filled with trees and a thin mother of one who liked to work at her clothesline because it felt closer to heaven.

Marva had been at the line when the chaplain arrived, and she didn't need to hear his message to know she'd never get another phone call from her son. She collapsed in the yard and pulled her apron up to her face, muffling the unique screams that only a mother of a dead soldier is entitled to make. The screams started from the gut, from the place the soldier came from, and grew, just like he did, getting louder and longer and stronger until they burst out on their own and took flight.

John heard the screams from the shower and came running in a robe, his wet hair stuck to his forehead. He knelt in front of her beneath the clothesline and pulled her to his chest. He made promises that even he didn't yet believe. He spoke in a single long breath, a whispered rambling run-on monologue, promising that J.R. was better now, closer to God, cloaked with eternal honor, unafraid, without pain or worry.

Marva hoped it was true. Later, she knew it was true. But the knowledge didn't erase how much she missed her son or the man who'd insisted all would be well.

12:05 P.M.

Marva's eyes shot open on the first ring.

"Hello?"

"Marva?"

"Yes."

"This is Emily."

"Hello." Marva pushed herself up with one arm and grimaced. "Is everything all right?"

"Yes, but I'm calling about you. Are you okay?"

"Of course. My. Of course. Just tired today."

Marva switched the phone from one ear to the other. "How's our Charlee?"

"The same. She's the same. She asked about you. She misses you."

"My. I'm sorry. I've been tired a day or two, I suppose. I'll make it by for a visit. I miss her, too."

"Do you need anything?" Emily asked. "Can we come by? I'm here with Charlee, but I could send Zach. He's home. Should I do that?"

"No, no. I'm fine. Just slow today, that's all. I'll come by later today, please tell Charlee. And I'll bring more balloons."

"She'd like that. Would you mind bringing Zach with you? If you come? No pressure, of course. But Thomas is working today out of town, and Zach is stuck home alone on a Saturday."

"Of course. I'll stop there on my way."

The women said good-bye, and Marva finally inched toward the edge of the bed. She looked at the clock a final time. She wished it read 6:17.

14
Visitors

Zach walked home from Miss Marva's in a tightening spiral, gradually losing pace, uneasy about a direct approach, like a plane with a broken wing. He considered that if his engine ran any slower, he might stall and crash.

He stopped at the tree stump Charlee loved, the one he saw her on from the trailer's back window. Part of him wanted to stand on it, too. To see if it really made him into someone different the way it did for his sister. He wondered: would it make him taller? But instead of standing on it, he circled it like he had the patches of noxious weeds that were once dandelions.

The afternoon at Miss Marva's felt like beating the high score on his favorite video game. He'd been treated like a VIP; he'd been listened to. Miss Marva sat through a detailed description of how to play *Call of Duty* and promised one day to come by for a demonstration of *Guitar Hero*.

Miss Marva looked him in the eye, and Zach had noticed. He enjoyed the pictures and the stories about her son in the war, and he wished, just for her, that he would have come home alive. She seemed to enjoy Zach's stories, too, many of them about Charlee and their life before Woodbrook.

She'd asked Zach to fix some lights that had burned out around her Christmas tree, and while he tested and retested the strands, she sat on the couch and described some of the many ornaments from a distance. Later, when she'd described the significance of the Advent calendar on the mantel, he'd only pretended to be interested. But by the time she was done, he was tuned in with eyes open and curiosity piqued.

He even looked through Miss Marva's aprons when she'd asked if he'd help her find the specific one she wanted to wear. He would never personally wear one. "Totally not ever," he'd told her, but he had to admit that a few of them made him LOL. This, of course, led to a text and instant messaging lesson. *She was fascinated,* he thought, *like a real friend.* He promised to come back one day with a cheat sheet for her.

Before he'd left, while sitting at the opposite end of the couch drinking the hot chocolate he'd made at Miss Marva's request, she had asked the simple question: "Would you tell me about your old school?"

"Um . . ." The answer stalled like the rusty VW Beetle in his yard. "I don't know. . . . It was . . . It was like whatever . . ."

"Whatever what?"

"I didn't fit in. Nobody really liked me there."

"Zach Alexander, that can't be true. I bet everyone liked you."

Zach snorted. "Not hardly. Nobody did. Plus my grades stunk. I'll never be as smart as Charlee." He fished with a spoon for a mini-marshmallow in his hot chocolate.

"My. I bet you my favorite apron that's not true."

"It is," he said, but without sadness or jealousy. "She's really smart, even for a little kid. I bet she gets straight A's for pretty much forever."

Zach didn't say it, but he hoped forever meant at least the rest of elementary school.

When they both had finished their hot chocolate, they said good-bye, and Zach took his time trekking home. When he arrived at the back door of the trailer, he heard his parents inside arguing. He sat on the step and listened to them fight about Christmas, money, his mother's job, his father's struggles to find steady work and be at the hospital at the same time, Charlee, Charlee's odds, Charlee's doctors, the hospital bills, other bills, and life insurance.

Zach thought they'd run dry of anger, but before any kind words came, they had zigzagged back into arguing about Christmas again, splurging on a real tree at home, getting a small tree for Charlee's room or skipping it altogether and just praying Charlee would come home.

The one thing he didn't hear, for once, was his own name.

Zach finally opened the door and walked in. Both parents looked at him, but neither really saw him, and he passed through to the room he shared with someone who hadn't slept there in more than two weeks.

For the first time since they'd moved to 27 Homes, he didn't just use her bed to climb up to his own. He stayed on hers, resting his head on her pillow and looking up at the bottom of his bunk.

The arguing from the next room grew louder, and he wished one of them would just walk out, slam the door if they had to, instead of making lists of every single worry out loud. They'd moved on from the day's problems to disagreeing and re-disagreeing about things from their old and easier life in a place he hardly remembered anymore.

He closed his eyes and wondered if Charlee was sleeping. He wondered, too, if Marva had gone to bed or if she'd remained on the couch where he'd left her, locking the door behind him.

Finally, with nothing else to do and no other excuses, he knelt on Charlee's bed and prayed to a God he wasn't sure had time to listen.

15
The *Woodbrook Weekly*

Woodbrook's Odd Couple
by Rusty Cleveland

It is the most unusual friendship.

One is pint-sized, just nine years old and full of life. But she's not full of life lived; she's full of dreams and a life yet to live.

The other has already lived a beautiful life. At the age of eighty-one, she wonders just where the finish line is and at what speed she'll cross it.

One spent most of her autumn school days watching the classroom clock and waiting for the sound of that final bell so she could get home and skip her way across the weedy patch of ground between her home and that of her best friend's.

The other has done much the same thing. She has eyed the kitchen clock and willed it along, minute by minute, eager to hear the roar of the yellow bus making its way through the neighborhood.

They are Charlee and Marva. The former is an old soul in the innocent body of a child. The latter is a young soul in the tired body of a widow. Their differences complement their extraordinary bond.

Marva collects aprons and has hundreds of them folded nicely in drawers and arranged on hooks and pegs around her home. One of my personal favorites reads "If you want breakfast in bed, sleep in the kitchen." She wears several throughout the day as part of her regular outfit. To see her without one is almost like seeing a turtle without its shell.

Charlee? Well, Charlee collects days and prays her collection will eventually grow into the years of a long life.

On Thanksgiving Day, Marva had a crowded house for dinner in a home that looked so much like Christmas, she could be sued for copyright infringement. Joining her around the festive dinner table were Charlee Alexander and her family. In the midst of this picture-perfect gathering, something went terribly wrong. A brain tumor spoiled the party. A brain tumor disrupted lives. It was an evening these two friends will never forget.

What began with a prayer at the dinner table ended with prayers at Woodbrook Mercy Hospital that

Charlee would survive the tumor that lurked near the back of her brain. It's impossible to know how long it has been waiting for attention, silently hinting at danger with headaches and stomachaches that are often part of an active child's life.

Charlee's doctors are some of the finest to ever don scrubs and white coats. Correction: Charlee suggests that her doctors don't wear coats. They wear capes.

Because Charlee has avoided the most common post-surgery complications, her family will bring her home today, just eighteen days since their lives changed.

Charlee will be weak, but she will be home. She will continue her radiation and chemotherapy, but she will be home.

It's easy to imagine our little heroine, once settled and rested, making that walk, maybe even with a hint of a skip in her step, across the field from her house to visit her best friend. She'll sit and smile with approval at the newest addition to Marva's apron collection and swim in the sweet smells of cranberry-scented candles and Christmas fudge. The two friends will laugh. And then laugh some more.

Charlee will not yet grasp how fortunate she is that the doctors are confident they removed the entire tumor. But Marva will, and the thought will bring tears to her eyes that Charlee will try to will away. It's not the finish line that is on Marva's mind so much these days, but the race of life itself and the longing to spend even one more day with her pint-sized, precious friend.

There is not a person reading this today who hasn't been touched by cancer. It is a disease with a wide and deep family tree that does not discriminate. It takes the elderly, those who've already lived through the aches and pains. It attacks the young, like Charlee, who only pray they will experience the aches and pains of growing old.

Cancer can make a loud, grand entrance, the way it did for Charlee, and give us a fighting chance to beat it.

Or it can come on stage silently, doing its damage in the unswept edges of the theater, not stepping into the spotlight until the only option is to get comfortable until the show is over.

Today, eleven families across America will learn their child has a spinal cord or brain tumor. Three more families will say good-bye to their child; such funerals can break the strongest men and often wedge families apart into pieces that cannot be reassembled.

Think of it: between now and Christmas morning, 150 families will discover that their child, the one who, days ago, dreamed of playing professional football, or dancing on Broadway, or sailing around the world, or curing cancer, now only dreams of being alive on Christmas morning.

Some of these cancer patients will have strong family teams behind them: coaches, doctors, teammates, siblings, cheerleaders, and friends. The lucky ones will have a Marva.

Others will have nothing and no one, only the fear that comes from leaving the world before anyone notices they're even gone.

No matter the size of the team or the depth of the bench, these are frightening days for a cancer patient. Memories of happy, healthy holidays are crowded out by fears that this one could be the last. Those fears lead us to live with cameras in our eyes, capturing every colorful detail while we pray to replace them with happier memories next year, but knowing what we see today may become the anchor memories of our shared lives.

What about you? Is there a Charlee in your life? Do you know someone struggling with cancer or some other illness this Christmas? Do you know someone who is perfectly healthy but who feels imperfect and lonely? Is there a team that needs you? Someone you can serve?

Who do you know who is facing days of Christmas that seem destined to be bleak when they should be bright, foggy when they should be fearless, full of loneliness when they should be full of love?

Charlee and Marva, together, are unwrapping each new day as if it is a gift. They're experiencing what it truly means to make every day count. It's a message of Christmas we all can take to heart.

No, not everyone has a friend like Marva at their side. But just think of those who can have a friend in you.

16
Homecoming

Today's the day," Nurse Becky Reynolds said. "Can you believe it's here?"

No, Charlee couldn't. She'd seen nothing for weeks except for her hospital room and a few short green and white hallways on her floor. She'd walked up and down those shiny hallways, pulling an IV with Melvin the monkey perched precariously on top.

She missed her home.

She missed the other twenty-six, too.

She missed the neighbors who hardly spoke to her. She missed watching the boys climb and tumble down the dirt and gravel pile at the end of the short barb street. She wanted to wave to the porch rockers, walk down the street for no reason, and turn around and wave again, just because she could.

Charlee couldn't wait to lie in her own bed and stare up at Zach's bunk and know she wasn't the only one in the room. She missed his music being turned up so loud she could hear the buzzing and booming sneaking out from his earbuds.

But mostly, she missed Miss Marva. She'd been to visit Charlee every few days, but was never able to stay long. She hoped her friend wouldn't be too tired for another visit, and that Charlee wouldn't be too tired to host her.

"What's the first thing you'll do?" Nurse Becky asked as she made notes on Charlee's chart.

"I don't know. There's a lot on my list. I never even got to finish my Thanksgiving turkey dinner."

"I betcha you'll get that chance, Charlee."

"I hope it's a different turkey!"

Nurse Becky laughed and slid the chart back into a wall pocket. "I hope so, too," she said and she sat on the edge of Charlee's bed. "Your mom and dad are with the doctor right now going over your schedule. But since it's just you and me, can I share a secret with you?"

"Sure." Charlee wrapped Melvin's long arms around his head until they doubled back over his ears.

"It's really, really important that you rest at home. I know you want to do everything, but it's super important that you take it slow. You're going to be coming back a lot for treatments, and they're going to make you very tired. So you need to save your energy as much as you can. Like a dessert you want to last a long time. Understand?"

"I think so."

"How about this. You like movies?"

"Uh-huh."

"Maybe just picture yourself in slow motion, like they do in the movies sometimes. When you feel like eating too fast, or walking too fast from the bedroom to your bathroom, or wherever, just imagine you're in a movie going suuuuper sloooow. Can you do that for me?"

"I can try."

"Promise?"

"Promise," Charlee said, as she wrapped her pinkie around Nurse Becky's.

Charlee rode in the middle seat of the minivan and clutched a fat pillow, a gift from Nurse Becky that the other nurses and doctors had signed and drawn smiley faces on in brightly colored permanent markers.

Her dad drove and her mother rode in the passenger's seat, but she spent so much time turned around looking at her daughter, Charlee thought she should have just sat next to her.

"How you feeling?" Emily asked.

"Good."

"Not sick?"

"Nope."

"You'll tell me?"

"Yep."

"All right."

They drove slowly from the hospital through Woodbrook and Charlee pointed out the town's Christmas decorations that hadn't been there the last time she'd been downtown.

"There's a wreath on every streetlight!" Charlee said.

"Isn't it nice?"

"Uh-huh. Drive slower, Dad."

Emily turned again as they neared the entrance for 27 Homes and put her hand on Charlee's knee. "Remember everything we've talked about, right?"

"Yes, Mom."

"You're still a little sick, sweetheart, and we still have a long ways to go. Lots of trips back for treatments to make sure the big sickness doesn't come back. That means we have to be careful."

"I know."

"No playing outside. It's bed, the couch, and short times at the table, for now."

"I know, Mom."

"And we know you want to visit Marva, but not yet. Not until the doctor says it's all right."

"I know," Charlee said, a hint of irritation creeping into her voice.

"She knows, Emily," Thomas said. "Right, Charlee Chew?"

Charlee saw her dad wink at her in the rearview mirror. "Uh-huh."

"We've got a few surprises in store," her dad said, looking back again. "How does that sound?"

"You do?"

"We sure do," he added. "Christmas is all about surprises, right?"

They pulled into the neighborhood, and Charlee grinned at the sight of a wreath capped with a bright red bow hanging from the front door of their trailer.

The wreath, Charlee soon learned, was only the beginning. The trailer had been "Christmased," as Charlee called it. Lights draped from the cabinets in the kitchen, a motion-sensor dancing Santa stood on the counter next to the toaster, and Miss Marva's large tree towered in the corner of the snug living room. The tree stretched so far into the room it left little space around it for anything but the TV stand and a recliner.

Even Zach was in the holiday mood. They found him sitting at the table wearing a green cotton elf hat with a jingly brass ball hanging from the end.

"I have a gift for you," he said.

"You do?"

Zach reached under the table and pulled up a box wrapped in the local newspaper. "Sorry it's not real wrapping paper. I didn't think about it until you were already on the way back."

Charlee was so happy to be home, to see Zach and to have something waiting with her name on it, she would have been content if the gift hadn't been wrapped at all.

"Thanks, Zach," she said. "Can I open it now?"

He nodded and she ripped at the top of the wrapping, quickly exposing the box and freeing it from the newspaper.

"Miss Marva sorta helped buy them," Zach said.

Charlee spun the box around to examine the picture of a pair of florescent yellow, two-way radios. "Are these walkie-talkies?"

"Sorta," Zach said. "They're pretty much the nicest you can get around here. Like I said, Miss Marva chipped in."

Charlee pulled off a piece of tape and opened the box. She pulled out a Styrofoam block with two spaces, but only one radio. "Where's the other one?"

Zach took the packaging from her, removed the radio, and turned it on. "Say something," he said, holding down the button.

Charlee took it from him and looked curiously at her father.

"Go ahead," Thomas said. "Say something."

Charlee put her lips close to the front of the radio. "Hello?" But she didn't release the button until Zach gingerly slid her finger off it.

No response.

"Try again," Zach said. "And remember to only press the button while you're talking. You have to let go to hear the other person."

Charlee pushed the button and pressed her lips right against the radio. "Hello? Is anyone there?"

"Charlee!" The voice came through without any pops or crackles.

Charlee giggled. "Who is this?"

"My. Well, who do you think it is?"

For the first time in weeks, Charlee's smile was almost as wide as Melvin's. "Miss Marva!" she squealed, but then forgot to release the button and Zach again reached over and nudged her finger.

"Good guess, dear. It's your favorite neighbor from across the field."

"You're my favorite neighbor anywhere," Charlee said, and she immediately released the button, drawing a thumbs-up from her brother.

"How are you feeling today?" Miss Marva asked.

"I'm good. How are you doing? I miss you. I'm home now."

"I know you're home, dear." Charlee could hear Miss Marva laughing. "And I'm very happy about that."

"Me too. But Mom says I can't leave to visit you for a while."

"I know—that's why Zach got these for us. You can talk to me anytime."

"Anytime?"

"If I'm awake, you can talk to me whenever you like. I'll leave it on and in my apron pocket all day."

"Thanks!"

"You'll listen to your folks, right? Do what they say and get better soon?"

"I will."

"And I'll come visit when I can. And soon, I promise, you can come back over to my house."

"Okay," Charlee said, but she immediately hit the button again. "Wait! Thanks for loaning us your tree! It takes up the whole house!"

"I'm so glad."

The two friends chatted back and forth for another minute while Charlee's parents unloaded her things from the van.

"I like talking to you, but I wish I could see you, too," Charlee said.

After a beat of silence, Marva's voice came back across the radio. "How about you count to ten and then look out your window at my back porch. Can you see that far?"

"Sure I can! One . . . two . . . three . . . four . . . five . . ." Charlee quickened the pace. "Six, seven, eight, nine, ten!" Then she got up from the table and looked out the back door.

Marva stood on her front porch waving with both arms and wearing an apron.

Charlee pressed the radio button. "Hi! What does your apron say?"

"It says: Welcome home, Charlee."

17
Doubting Thomas

Thomas sat in the dark. On the floor, a portable space heater's digital display tried to convince him it was 65 degrees. Thomas knew better. A December cold front had settled in the south, and Woodbrook was getting its first taste of winter.

At 5:15 in the morning, wind lashed against the thin walls of the trailer like waves on a sea wall. He was grateful Emily and the kids could sleep through it, but Thomas wondered how they possibly could. If he really considered it, he hadn't slept well since moving to 27 Homes. But cold, unkind nights like the last one only made it harder for him to turn off his mind and hand it over to the night.

He poured a second, smaller bowl of cereal and finished it quickly. Then, for the third time that morning, he checked on Charlee. She slept soundly under a sheet and two blankets, clutching Melvin with one arm and the top blanket with another. She wore a knit cap on her head, and her face was partially obscured by her pillow. Still, from Thomas's view in the doorway, it looked like she was almost smiling.

He mouthed a good-bye to Zach and Charlee, shut the door, and made his way outside. *The wind has slowed,* he thought, but it still blew with enough personality to punish his ears. The hood was still up on the Beetle, and he stopped to admire his work using his cell phone as a flashlight. One of Thomas's friends from a job site had offered to let Thomas raid his own comatose VW for parts in exchange for help framing a basement. With Zach's help, he'd made enough progress that the engine was finally turning over.

Thomas looked in the driver's side window and blew into his hands. The car still lacked seat belts, and Thomas knew he'd need to get them installed before Emily would let him take Zach for a ride, even around their quiet neighborhood.

The seat belts weren't the only things missing. The car had no working emergency brake and no windshield wipers. Only one headlight worked—even though the bulbs were new. At least the wiper motor successfully moved the stubby metal brackets back and forth in rhythm through the air. It was a start.

Thomas carefully and quietly lowered and latched the hood. He noticed Marva's lights on across the field, and he checked the time on his cell phone: 5:33. He wished he had more time and could check on the only neighbor the family really knew, but he faced a twenty-minute drive to work and an early start time. Later, if he remembered, he'd text Emily and ask if she'd check on Marva before taking Charlee in for her treatment.

He climbed in his clunker truck and lifted the handle with both hands to shut the door. It was his daily ritual to miss the bells and whistles of the beefy Ford F-250 he'd left on the dealership lot when he could no longer make his payments.

The other truck was made-in-America strong and made him feel successful; the clunker was foreign and made him feel like he was cheating on his country.

The other truck had seat warmers; the clunker had seats.

The other truck had satellite radio; the clunker had a radio that worked when Thomas rolled down the window and held on to the makeshift antenna that had been duct taped to the side of the truck.

It was strange, he knew, but he thought the other truck smelled like leather and hard work; the clunker smelled like tuna fish and failure.

Thomas pulled out of 27 Homes and onto the rural highway that ran into town. He passed only two cars on the short drive between the neighborhood and the first of six traffic lights on Main Street. Downtown was quiet, too, and only a few cars lit the air with headlights and turn signals onto the town's narrow side streets. He sat at the first light and admired a dark red, antique Chevy truck sitting in the parking lot of Oakli's Barely

Owned Cars. The light changed and by the time he noticed, it was already turning yellow.

He rolled through but was stopped again at the second light. "Figures," he said aloud. "Nobody around, and I'm on the wrong side of the cycle." On his left, the lights were already bright at Utley Dental Care, and he wondered who trusted a sleepy dentist to go spelunking in their mouth at 6:00 A.M.

At the third light he stopped again, but he would have run it if not for the two town cops standing outside Shrum's bakery and coffee shop. He also noticed a new craft store called Jadi's and hoped Charlee would one day browse its aisles.

The fourth light also stopped him, and he noticed for the first time a sign on the door of a two-story brick building that read *Woodbrook Sleep Clinic—Dr. Sammi Denson.* He found it ironic their lights were on that early, too.

At the fifth light, which seemed to last longer than three Sunday sunrises, Thomas cursed under his breath when a county sheriff's deputy cruiser approached the intersection and stopped. When they finally passed each other, Thomas thought the deputy eyeballed him like a guilty man.

At the sixth and final light on Woodbrook's Main Street, Thomas found himself sitting in front of the Woodbrook town offices where he had first picked up the keys to a dirty trailer in a dirty neighborhood. He wished he could pull in and return the keys to the assistant town manager, the one who'd signed their rental contract. Could he slide the keys across the counter and drive in reverse back to their former lives, their former selves? Could he rewind it all? The move? Bankruptcy? Charlee's cancer?

The wind picked up again in an insistent, angry tantrum, and a wreath on the door of Starnes' Salon blew off its hook and rolled like a tire across the intersection. Pieces of pine branches and holly peeled from the wreath; the bow untied, but did not detach. By the time it came to rest against a newspaper box, it wasn't a wreath anymore. It was nothing more than a collection of battered branches with a tattered bow.

Thomas stared at it through the light cycle until the car behind him honked and delivered him back from the wreath to the present.

A project foreman met Thomas in the parking lot of the new sixteen-unit apartment building they'd been working on for two weeks. "No work today, sorry, Thomas."

"What do you mean no work?"

"I mean we don't need you on this job anymore. You're done. We're ahead of schedule."

"What about paint?"

"It's covered. Same crew from the motel remodel."

"Flooring?"

"Guys are coming for that next week, if we're ready."

"Come on, man, I need this. There must be something."

"Sorry, Thomas. Call the office in a few days, see if something else pops on another job." The foreman nodded another apology and turned his back.

Thomas dropped his head onto the window of his truck. The sky had begun to stroke from black to blue and the light mixed with the yellow from the parking lot lamp overhead. Thomas pulled his head back and examined his unshaven reflection. But it wasn't his face he saw; it was Charlee's.

Inside the truck but still sitting in the unfinished, unpaved parking lot, he let his temperature rise to a boil, and he banged both fists against the steering wheel until the faux leather cover came loose and hung half off. He ripped it off with a single, violent yank and slapped it against the dash until the radio turned on and the knob popped off.

He punched the radio once with the bottom of his clenched right fist, and the static disappeared as quickly as it arrived.

"My God."

Thomas gripped the cold wheel and rocked his head back against the headrest.

"My God. Is this real, God?"

He breathed out, loosened his tight grip, and began to knead the curve of the wheel.

"Is this really my life now, God? Is it?"

For the first time all morning, and despite having the heater running in the clunker since he'd left for work, Thomas noticed he could see his breath against the December morning. "Are you paying attention? At all? Where are you?" He inhaled and said the words much louder a second time. "Where are you?"

Thomas closed his eyes. "God, Heavenly Father, Lord, whatever. I'm trying here. I'm doing my best. Do you not see that? Am I not trying?" He paused, as if expecting an answer from a debate partner. "Listen. We need you. Mostly Charlee needs you. But probably Zach, too. The whole family needs you to notice us and pitch in. Could you please pitch in, God? Please?"

Thomas started the truck and re-gripped the wheel. "How about a sign? Huh? Something that says we're not completely forgotten down here in this hole of a life. Something that says loud and clear you know what we're going through, that we're trying to make it here."

Thomas didn't know how much time had passed while he waited. He only knew the sun was up, and he'd stopped praying.

18
What's Your Twenty?

Miss Marva?"

No response.

"Miss Marva, hello?"

Charlee counted to thirty and tried again. "Miss Marva, are you there?"

"Hello, Charlee, I'm here."

"Hi!" Charlee shouted into the walkie-talkie. "What's your twenty?"

"My twenty?"

"Zach says that means where are you right now."

"Oh, of course, my twenty. My twenty is in bed, I'm afraid."

"But it's lunchtime."

"I know, sweetheart. I couldn't sleep and got up very early. Then I guess I wore out and decided to lay back down."

"Did I wake you up? I'm sorry."

"No, I was just laying here in bed. But not sleeping."

"Promise?"

"I promise."

"What apron are you wearing today?"

"I'm not wearing one today. I must have forgotten."

Charlee sat up in her own bed and exchanged a glance with Melvin. "You forgot? But you never forget."

The reply took its time, but just when Charlee was about to try again, the walkie-talkie squawked. "Enough about me forgetting. I want to know about you. What's *your* twenty?"

"Bed. My twenty is in bed, too. It stinks."

"I'm sorry, Charlee. How are you feeling?"

"I'm tired, too. But I'm always tired right now. The doctor said that's part of the treatments." She released the talk button and took off her knit cap. She pulled a clump of hair from inside and hit the button again. "I'm losing my hair, Miss Marva."

"I'm really sorry, sweetheart. Just think how lovely it will look when it grows back."

"That's what Mom says."

"And she's right."

Charlee ran her fingers through her hair and dark strands stuck to her fingers as if they had been covered in honey. "Guess what? The doctor said it might grow back different. Like a different color or more curly."

"I didn't know that."

"Me neither. But curly might be nice to try. I could be a brand-new Charlee Alexander."

"Oh, sweetheart. No matter if your hair falls out or how it grows back, you'll always be the same Charlee."

Charlee sat on the edge of her bed and wondered what pajamas Miss Marva was wearing. She pictured her hair, her face, the hallway connecting her room to the main portion of her house. She wondered what the empty space in the living room looked like without the tree filling it.

"Miss Marva, do you miss your tree?"

"Not really. I think the tree needed you this year."

"Don't you mean we needed the tree?"

"I mean you needed each other."

Charlee sighed and wiggled her toes inside a pair of her dad's oversized socks. "It must be lonely there. Have you had any visitors?"

"My. Yes. Zach stops by every day after school to check on me. And your mother comes by sometimes, too."

"Do you make them wear aprons?"

Charlee heard Marva laugh. "No, but I should, shouldn't I?"

"At least Mom."

"Consider it done. I'll have one ready next time she comes." Another silent minute passed. "I've had a few ladies from the library come by, too. Just to say hello. And my friend, Rusty—remember him?"

"The man from the newspaper."

"That's right. He's been by to check on me. He even

offered to get me a small tree, one to go on the table, like Charlie Brown had."

Charlee smiled. "I love that tree."

"Me too."

Charlee stood but the floor seemed to shift under her. She supported herself against Zach's bunk before slowly lowering herself back to the edge of her own bed.

"How about you, Charlee? Have you had any visitors?"

"Just Nurse Becky. She says I can't really have any other visitors or I'll get an infection. If my temperature gets hot, they have to take me back to the hospital. Even a little bit warm, Mom says."

"I see."

"That stinks, too."

"I know it does. . . . What about Mom and Dad? Where are they today?"

"Dad is at work, I think. Mom is in the kitchen on the phone. She's trying to find a second job."

"I see."

"Zach's at school." Charlee looked at Melvin. "I wish I could go to school."

"You'll go again, don't worry."

Charlee pulled her legs under her and sat cross-legged in the middle of her bed. "Are you getting ready for Christmas? It's coming fast, you know."

"I know it is. But you already helped me get ready. Remember spending the day here before Thanksgiving?"

"Yeah. That was a good day."

"My. It sure was."

"Have you bought any presents?"

"A few."

"Where are they? Since you don't have a tree, where are you keeping them?"

"You think of everything, don't you, Charlee? I put them by the calendar."

Charlee let the answer hang. "Oh." She wanted to ask if there were any presents with her name on them, but she thought seeing Miss Marva again before Christmas would be enough of a gift. Still, Charlee decided to keep that to herself, just in case she got both.

"We have a couple of gifts under our tree—I mean *your* tree."

"That's nice."

Charlee set the walkie-talkie down and pulled her knit cap back on. "It's cold outside. Have you been outside?"

"Not really."

Charlee lay down and tucked Melvin in next to her. "Melvin says hi."

"Tell him hi back. And tell him that I miss him."

"He says he misses you more." Charlee lay quietly a moment. "Are you still tired, Miss Marva?"

"I sure am."

"Me too."

A few more minutes passed as Charlee stared at the bottom of Zach's bunk. "We should take a nap."

"That's a good idea."

"You'll keep your walkie close?"

"I will."

"Okay."

Charlee let another moment pass. "I love you, Miss Marva."

"I love you too, Charlee."

THE NOTE

DECEMBER 13

Dear Charlee:

Surprise! We hope you found our note tonight without any problems. We weren't sure exactly where to leave it, but if you're reading this, we must have done all right.

Before we go any further, we want you to know that this letter, and the other items that will follow, are for you. But because we know how special you are, we also know you might want to share with your family. That would be just fine with us.

Now, without further ado, please allow us to introduce ourselves. We are a family of Traveling Elves, very unusual elves, and we've got a story to tell about the popular song "The 12 Days of Christmas."

We are sure you know the song, but did you know that we wrote it?

It's true! There are many theories about the song's origin, but we know the truth because our family wrote every word. Unfortunately, some of the verses have been misunderstood or translated incorrectly. So this year, finally, we shall clear a few things up!

Curious yet, Charlee? There's more! We can't wait to reveal to you the lost 13th Day of Christmas. It's a mysterious thirteenth verse that has remained a secret . . . until now!

Yes, after countless hours of serious elf deliberation,

we are very pleased to have found and chosen you, Charlee Alexander!

We've wanted to share these mysteries before, but we simply couldn't find the right person. But you couldn't be more perfect, Charlee. And once you learn our secret, we just might give you permission to share it with someone else. We'll see!

Beginning tomorrow evening, we will deliver to you gifts representing each of the 13 Days of Christmas. We will also include our top secret daily travel log for your records.

We hope this brings you a bit of holiday cheer. Traveling the globe in our sleigh and collecting these items has been such a joy for us. (Except, of course, for the immunizations, the horrible sleigh food, and having to go through customs all the time. But we'll get to that.)

Finally, and this is important for you and your entire family, please do not try to catch us in the act. We wish to remain anonymous. We know that as the days unfold between now and Christmas, you might be tempted to peek out the window, or hide in the bushes, or use a satellite to track our sleigh. But Charlee, the mystery must remain!

Let the 12—we mean the 13—Days of Christmas begin!

Love,
The Traveling Elves

19
Sherlock Charlee

"Canyoubelieveiteverybody?" Charlee rattled the words so quickly they sounded like one. Then she took a giddy, childlike gulp of air and said it again more slowly, punching each word as if standing on stage and speaking to the last row of the upper balcony.

"It's really something, isn't it, Charlee Chew?" Thomas stood at the kitchen sink, scrubbing engine grease from his calloused hands.

Charlee still stood by the trailer's front door holding the letter by the edges with her fingertips. She wore her pink-and-white Disney long johns with the silhouettes of princesses. "Tell me exactly how you found it, Daddy." She eased the letter further into the air and away from her body. It was evidence and she didn't want to taint it with her own prints.

Her father turned off the running water and leaned against the counter. He smiled at Emily and Zack who were sitting at the kitchen table eating the scattered remnants of the family's everything-goes nachos. "I came home, like you know, and I noticed the envelope on the doormat. I picked it up and started to open the door, then remembered I wanted to check something on the Beetle that I didn't finish last night. So I stuck it in my back pocket and went back out to the car. And I yelled at Zach to help for a minute."

Charlee noticed her father's eyes went from hers to her mother's.

"And we got carried away. It's pretty warm out there, nice weather, right? I guess we stayed out there longer than I realized."

"Sounds right to me," Charlee's mother said as she scooped a stray clump of black beans onto a broken tortilla chip.

"So then we came in, handed you the envelope, and I started washing my hands."

"In the kitchen," Emily said. "You washed your hands in my kitchen sink."

"Yeah, sorry about that. Zach was using the bathroom sink."

Charlee read the letter again—aloud. She'd inched it off her fingertips but still clung to it with her nails. "I wonder how long it's been there. I wonder if they walked up to the house or drove. Why me? When did you go outside the front door last? Was it there when you got home from work at Walmart, Mom?

Has anyone seen Miss Marva driving around today? Are her lights on? Where's my walkie-talkie?"

"Easy, Charlee," her mother said. "Aren't you supposed to just be happy with the surprise? Isn't that what it says?"

"I guess so, but it's so exciting, isn't it?" Charlee moved to the table, sat in her usual spot, and carefully refolded and reinserted the letter into the plain white envelope. Her name was scrawled on the front in blue ink. "It's definitely not Miss Marva's writing though, definitely not. I've seen hers before. This isn't hers." Charlee's mind was spinning. "Is it because we're poor?"

"We're not poor," Charlee's dad barked.

"Zach says we are." Charlee looked across the table at her brother, but his eyes were down as he scraped cooled cheese from the large plate that once held dinner.

"He's wrong," Thomas said.

"Is it because of the cancer? Because I'm sick?"

"You're not sick," Thomas said, and he pulled her knit cap down over her eyes. "You were, but you're fine now."

"You're getting better, Charlee." Her mother shifted the cap back above Charlee's eyes. "But yes, it could be because of all the excitement around here."

"Uh-huh," Charlee said, nodding. But she couldn't have repeated what her mother said. She took the letter back out of the envelope to read to herself again. When she was done, she returned it to its envelope and rested her head on her folded arms atop the table and faced her mother.

"Is it someone from Dad's work? Or maybe someone from Walmart. You said you've made friends there." Charlee's breathing became shallow. "Maybe it's the old waving ladies on the bend. Or someone from school. Or the neighborhood."

Her mother reached over and pulled off Charlee's cap. Charlee opened her eyes and saw a few strands of her thin hair fall through the air and land on the table. She closed her eyes again and felt her mother's hand gently caressing her balding head. Charlee could feel her mother's fingers closing together like a comb and capturing the few colonies of hair that remained like islands on a blotchy, peach-colored sea.

When she opened her eyes once more, her mother was also resting her head on the table, and Charlee thought her eyes looked wet. She whispered, "Don't worry, Mom. Even if I find out, I won't tell."

Charlee drifted a moment. She saw her mother's mouth move, but heard nothing. When she tried to whisper something back, she felt her words dying before they reached her lips.

Charlee heard nothing more that evening. Her mind was lost in aprons, calendars, and secrets.

DECEMBER 14

> *On the 1st Day of Christmas*
> *my true love sent to me:*
> *A Partridge in a Pear Tree*

Dear Charlee:

Our family wrote the first verse of our famous song while visiting the city of Rio de Janeiro, Brazil. But did you know that in our original draft, the first day didn't mention a partridge at all? It was only meant to be about a single, delicious pear.

Let us explain.

We were walking through a market and enjoying goodies of all kinds when we learned from a local farmer that Brazil has quite a reputation for growing some of the most sumptuous pears in the world. He was right! We noticed the color was perfect and the taste was heavenly. We knew right on the spot that the 1st Day of Christmas needed to be a pear tree. It was fate.

We toured orchard after orchard, sampling fruit and eyeing each tree with great care. We wanted the ideal tree to present on this 1st Day of Christmas. Nothing else would do for you!

At the last orchard of the day, just as daylight escaped over the westward mountains, standing on the edge of town and across the street from the local bus station, my sweet wife spotted the most gorgeous tree we'd ever seen. It was the tallest, the sturdiest, the best tree ever—precisely what we envisioned!

The kids and I began to dig it up while my wife sweet-talked the farmer into letting us have it. We planned to carefully bury the roots in a burlap sack and strap it tightly on the back of our sleigh.

But then, in an instant, history would be forever changed.

We noticed that at the bus station across the street, a shiny tour bus had pulled into the parking lot and a crowd of crazy teenage girls came rushing from every direction to greet it. As soon as the bus stopped, the door opened and a fine looking young man appeared.

Panicked and fear-stricken by the throngs of screaming girls, he jumped from the bus and cut a path straight through them. He darted across the street toward the orchard shouting, "Help me! Help me!" He was running right at us.

We were dumbfounded! Amazed! Bewildered! Flabbergasted! Overwhelmed! Startled! Stunned! Plus lots of other synonyms for surprised.

What should we do?

But before we could offer any assistance, the young man had climbed the very same pear tree we were trying to dig out of the ground.

We held off the screaming gaggle of girls, and eventually

they were shooed away by the young man's security team. But our new friend would not descend so quickly.

"Who are you?" I called up to him.

"You don't know?" he said.

"I'm sorry, we don't."

"I'm David Cassidy."

We chatted for nearly an hour before we could persuade him to climb down. He was so grateful for our help that he pitched in to dig up the tree and load it on the sleigh. We spent the evening talking and getting to know one another. By the time we said a tearful good-bye, we knew the first verse of our song needed to be slightly reworded in his honor.

So there you have it, the truth. Instead of just a "Pear Tree," it became a "Partridge in a Pear Tree."

Unfortunately, through the years of being lugged around, the tree died. But we want you to enjoy its final, tasty pear. It's an original!

Also, we're honored to present you with this CD. It's the greatest hits of our old friend, David Cassidy. You might not know who he is, but your parents probably do. Enjoy!

Happy 1st Day of Christmas!
The Traveling Elves

DECEMBER 15

On the 2nd Day of Christmas
my true love sent to me:
Two Turtle Doves

Dear Charlee:

There's no other way to say it, the story behind the Two Turtle Doves is a bit embarrassing. We wrote the verse a long time ago on a family journey to Papua, New Guinea, where we knew we could find the greatest variety of doves. But when the day arrived for the big trip, I developed a case of excessive ear wax and was ordered to bed for ten days. My wife and the little elves would have to go alone.

After two long days in the air, they arrived safely at the island and set off in search of your Two Turtle Doves. They knew just what they wanted. They even had a gold cage to put them in with a diamond-bedazzled water feeder mounted on the inside.

Before long, my wife succumbed to the scorching temperatures, and while she cooled off in the ice cream section of the local grocery store, the kids dug the cell phone out from the sleigh's glove box. They called me at home, filled me in on the latest news, and asked what they should do.

"Let Mom cool off while you go find the two urtle oves," I said on the other end of the phone.

"What, Papa?" the little ones answered back. "We can't hear you very well."

"Can you hear me now?" I said and moved by the window. "Can you hear me now?"

"Kinda. What are we to buy again?" the children screamed in unison into the phone.

"TWO URLE OVES!" I was growing a bit frustrated.

"Two urple oves?" the children replied.

"Yes! That's it!" I exclaimed, though I wasn't precisely sure I'd heard correctly. "Bring them home whenever Mom's cooled off."

The kids did as they thought they were told and bought two purple gloves.

The rest, as they say, is history. We all felt so bad about the mishap that we filled the gloves with candy to make up for the faulty cell phone reception. But at least they'll make a great tree ornament.

Enjoy your Two Purple Gloves! And whenever you sing the song in the future, you might consider singing the corrected lyrics.

Happy 2nd Day of Christmas!
The Traveling Elves

20
No Chances

Charlee's palms were sweating inside her two purple gloves.

"Maybe you should take them off while you sleep, sweetheart." Emily tugged on the blanket and tucked it down around Charlee's sides. "I think you'd sleep better."

"No, I'm okay." Charlee held her hands above her face, turning them over and over and admiring the pair of plain purple gloves that had appeared on her doorstep just hours earlier. "Aren't they so purple, Mom?"

Emily laughed. "Yes, sweetie, they're very purple. I'm glad they made you happy tonight."

Charlee rolled from her back to her side and interlocked her fingers, creating a fist pillow. She rested her head on it, her eyes locked on her mother.

Emily placed the back of her hand against Charlee's forehead.

"Hmm. You feel warm. I'm taking your temperature. Right back."

Charlee watched her mother step out of her bedroom. She leaned over the side of her bed and checked the power on her walkie-talkie. It sat on a plastic crate nightstand and a green light reassured her that Miss Marva wasn't far away.

Charlee missed her best friend. Even though disease and a browning winter field separated them, they'd been catching up each day, often chatting several times, but they hadn't been in the same room since Charlee had been in Woodbrook Mercy Hospital.

She was tired of hearing radio wave descriptions of Miss Marva's aprons. She wanted to see them for herself and help choose a spot for them on one of the many pegs and hooks.

She was tired of sending notes and drawings with Zach. They were nice, and Miss Marva usually sent back a note with a piece of candy or another surprise, but it wasn't the same, and she suspected her friend would agree.

More than anything, Charlee missed her friend's smile. It was big and wise. It made Charlee's heart think everything would be all right, even when her ears heard arguments that told her otherwise. It reminded her of the goofy, mega-smile plastered on Melvin's face, but she wasn't a little kid anymore. She loved Melvin, but she knew his smile wasn't by choice. It was by assembly line.

As much as she'd come to love Marva, Charlee had really grown to hate cancer. She'd learned words like chemotherapy, remission, and radiation. The big doctor words made her feel almost as sick as the drugs they gave her. The doctors had experimented with four different medications to help Charlee's upset stomach, but even the one they finally said was working didn't really make her stomach feel much better. It was still in knots.

Charlee looked up at the bottom of Zach's bunk. They rarely went to sleep at the same time anymore because she was forced to go to bed earlier than probably any kid in 27 Homes—maybe even earlier than any kid in all of Woodbrook.

Charlee imagined Zach sitting by the television and playing video games. She wished she could be sitting next to him watching him beat his high score or slay some evil enemy. Charlee would ask questions and cheer him on when he needed it, or encourage him to replay a level if he fell victim to a bad guy. Charlee knew those moments always made Zach happy, and Charlee liked to see him smiling.

Without looking, Charlee reached down to the nightstand and picked up the letter that came with her purple gloves. She read it once more and would have giggled again if she hadn't been so exhausted. *Miss Marva will never admit it,* she thought, but she was already convinced the 13 Days of Christmas must have been coming from her.

"Miss me?" Charlee's mother said, reentering the bedroom. Charlee's tired smile was her answer.

"Open up for the truth." Emily carefully slid the digital thermometer under Charlee's tongue and waited.

Charlee closed her eyes and willed her temperature down. She knew her parents called the thermometer "the truth" because she could fib about how she felt, but the digital readout could not.

They waited for the beep, and when it finally came, Charlee heard her mother take a deep breath as she pulled out the thermometer.

"Get dressed," she said in a burst. She ran from the room shouting, "Thomas, 100.4!"

For Charlee, time went from slow-trickle seconds to a white-water rush.

Charlee was in sweatpants.

Charlee was in the minivan.

Charlee was watching a confused Zach wave good-bye from behind the trailer's screen door.

Charlee was clutching Melvin with one arm and still wearing two purple gloves.

Charlee was in the emergency room, then an elevator, then the ICU.

Charlee was watching doctors gather and swarm over her as her temperature climbed.

Finally, lying in a bed that was not hers with a tube back in her arm, Charlee heard her mother's words separate themselves from the loud, messy current. "I am so sorry, Charlee."

She leaned in close. "The doctor said we just can't take any chances."

Charlee nodded and let her heavy eyelids win the night's long argument.

Emily kissed Charlee's forehead and whispered, "No chances."

DECEMBER 16

On the 3rd Day of Christmas
my true love sent to me:
Three French Hens

Dear Charlee:

Did you think we wouldn't find you in the hospital? Nice try!

It's true, we had to change our plans a bit to sneak past security, but we made it while you were napping. Never underestimate how close we are and how many others are watching you. Some you see, some you don't, but we're watching you and hoping you can go home soon.

On to Day Three!

After the shenanigans of the first two days, we were determined to get this one right. We traveled by sleigh to the heart of Paris, France, to find three genuine French hens for your gift.

The weather was warm, the cheese was soft, and the people were friendlier than usual. Ah, yes, it was a day to remember!

We happened across a little bakery tucked in the shadow of the Eiffel Tower. In the kitchen were Three French Hens working hard at the afternoon batch of hot bread and singing a lovely sounding song. Of course, we didn't understand the words, but nevertheless, we could tell they worked in perfect harmony.

Thankfully they could speak English. We made our pitch and asked if they would like to be part of history by being your gifts for this 3rd Day of Christmas. They were thrilled! They took off their aprons and joined us in the sleigh. All was right in the universe. That is, until we were airborne.

We were not ten miles outside of Paris before we heard whimpering in the backseat.

"I miss the bakery," one of the hens said.

"Me, too. I'm lonely," another followed in a thick French accent.

"Is it too late to turn back?" the third hen asked loudly.

My sweet wife turned to me and suggested the Three French Hens were too homesick to leave their beloved homeland. "We should turn around. We can't do this to them."

I muttered under my breath, "Chickens."

"No, dear—hens."

We returned them to their bakery. To make up for their change of heart, they gave us this gift of four beautiful loaves of French bread. They called it "Buy Three, Get One for the Tree."

Happy 3rd Day of Christmas!
The Traveling Elves

DECEMBER 17

On the 4th Day of Christmas
my true love sent to me:
Four Calling Birds

Dear Charlee:

Let's be honest. You were probably not expecting these kinds of birds. It's true, we've spent years trying to explain to well-meaning folks all over the world that we never meant live calling birds that fly. I mean, how original would that have been? And yet despite our best efforts, this Christmas, all over the world, people are thinking of four singing birdies when they sing our song. It's a shame.

But tonight, the misunderstandings end once and for all!

The truth is that while we were writing the fourth verse, we had a run of bad luck, and my wife had to take a side job in Los Angeles to help the family get by. She worked the phones as a telemarketer selling circus tickets. She made hundreds of calls a day and was quite good at it. In fact, she climbed up the corporate ladder and became head trainer of all new telemarketers.

One day, her boss pulled her aside and warned her that an unusual and challenging group of trainees was starting that day. They were a bunch of starving artists, divas, and aspiring actors, and they all were trying to find their big break in Hollywood. In the meantime, they needed some extra work to pay the bills. She would have to manage their supersized egos very carefully.

She walked into the conference room to meet the newbies and couldn't believe her eyes. They were an odd assortment indeed! They went around the room and intro-duced themselves.

"Hi, I'm Big Bird."

"My name is Woodstock."

"Call me Tweetie."

"Meep meep, Road Runner."

She looked past the feathers and learned to love all four birds. She took them under her . . . um . . . wing . . . if she had one . . . uh . . . you know what I mean.

She wanted them to pursue their dreams and even helped them land auditions with some of Hollywood's hot-test producers.

The rest, as they say, is history. All four birds went on to have big careers in television. Some continue acting even today. But we hope you never forget how they got their start—as four calling birds.

So, Charlee, tonight we're happy to present you with these four small stuffed animals. We wanted to have the real Big Bird, Woodstock, Tweetie, and Road Runner show up and meet you personally, but they're shooting a Christmas special.

Please enjoy your Four Calling Birds, and may you never again hear the song and think of four flying, messy, chirping birdies.

Happy 4th Day of Christmas!
The Traveling Elves

DECEMBER 18

On the 5th Day of Christmas
my true love sent to me:
Five Golden Rings

Dear Charlee:

Our spies tell us you're still under the weather at the hospital. Will you please get better soon? It's getting tough to sneak past the guards downstairs.

Speaking of hard to believe, the adventure behind the 5th day and verse is just that—hard to believe. Almost.

"Five Golden Rings"—easy enough, right? We spent a lot of time searching the globe for rings to match the song. We needed five special rings, each with its own significance.

Obviously we started our journey in space, choosing a ring from Saturn. No one seemed to notice it was missing, though we did have to retrofit the sleigh with a special trunk addition.

The second ring was from a small village in Africa called "Around the Collar." It wasn't as attractive as the Saturn ring, but it was definitely unique.

The third ring came from the "Lord of the Rings." We weren't sure if we made the right choice, but then one of the kids started cradling the ring in the backseat and mumbling "My precious," so we thought it must be special.

The fourth wring was found on the mysterious island of Yerneck. We'll let your mother explain why this one was so special.

The fifth and final ring came from the Olympic logo. Did you know there used to be six rings? We're hoping no one notices.

So that was it. We had our five glorious rings. They represented the fifth verse perfectly! All we had to do was drop them on your doorstep tonight.

Well, Charlee, a funny thing happened on our way to your neighborhood. You see, my wife needed to pick up some new toenail clippers at Walmart. While she sampled the latest models, I browsed the store, already looking ahead for tomorrow's items. And then I saw it . . .

It was an illuminated green display with white letters and a dash of red . . .

The smell was intoxicating, like fine, aged elf cheese—but better . . .

I approached and found a box of six small golden rings. I opened it and slowly pulled one of the rings from the box. It was soft, ever so sticky, and simply beautiful. I took a bite, then another and another, and soon everything around me seemed to turn in slow motion. That's why, to this day, verse five is sung more slowly than the rest and with extra gusto!

I looked at a man standing nearby. "What are these delicious rings?"

He answered with two of the tastiest words ever uttered in the history of the world: "Krispy Kremes."

I decided without a moment's hesitation that these rings needed to be yours. The rest of the family agreed, even though we had to eat a few more boxes of golden rings, just to be sure.

The famous rings we had gathered were donated to charity, and tonight we present to you a box of the real "Five Golden Rings." Please think of these when you sing the song hereafter and forevermore.

Happy 5th Day of Christmas!
The Traveling Elves

21
Just Waiting

Marva's eyes were fixed on the alarm clock: 6:16 A.M. When it buzzed at 6:17, she let the noise fill her bedroom until it chased off the silence. At 6:22, she turned it off and pushed herself up in bed.

She couldn't remember a time in her life when she'd been so tired. Not after doing laundry all day, not after cutting her own grass when she still could, not after staying up for days waiting for news from her son in Vietnam, not even when her husband was dying and, for weeks, Marva defeated sleep in a nightly battle.

Every limb ached. Marva felt each one, listening to them the way elderly people do. She waited for answers, but only heard what sounded like a debate about which leg hurt the most.

Marva wasn't hungry; her appetite had disappeared with Charlee's return to Woodbrook Mercy Hospital. If she really thought back in time, however, she wasn't sure she'd truly been hungry since Thanksgiving.

Marva looked at the walkie-talkie on her nightstand. It hadn't broadcast Charlee's voice in four days, but still she picked it up and turned it off and on again. If she didn't hear from Zach or Thomas or Emily by lunchtime, she'd use the walkie-talkie for an update and pretend it was Charlee on the other end.

Marva stretched her arms in front of her and the creaks sounded like a heavy man walking alone down a hardwood hallway. She hugged herself and bent forward until her spine begged her not to go further.

She put her hands at her sides and pushed up from the hard mattress, teetering on her feet a moment and using the headboard for balance. She breathed in deeply and shook her head to clear the gray colored white noise. Then Marva picked up the phone by the alarm clock and felt a breeze of relief at the sound of a dull dial tone.

Marva shuffled down the hallway in her long-sleeved night-gown. The house was cool, and Marva stopped at the thermo-stat in the living room to turn the temperature up. The kitchen floor was cold, and Marva considered going back to her room for socks, but she knew she'd be back on the other end of the house soon enough anyway.

She opened the curtains above the kitchen sink and looked

across the field to Charlee's trailer. A single light came from the kitchen window, and Marva imagined Thomas sitting at the table eating breakfast, or praying, or wondering how he and his family would make it through another day without Charlee's spirit replacing the sadness in their small home.

Marva remembered the apron she'd bought for Thomas as an early Christmas present and made a third—maybe fourth—mental note to give it to him when she had the energy.

Marva thought of Zach, too, hanging on to the final moments of sleep before waking for school where he would have to answer endless questions about his sick sister from teachers, friends, and the curious.

Marva sat and wondered where Emily had slept. Was she balled up on a waiting room couch? Had Charlee been moved from ICU and could Emily sleep in a second bed in her room? Marva began to offer a long prayer on behalf of all of the Alexanders, but then stopped and restarted, choosing instead to say a separate and powerful prayer for each, by name.

When she was done, she retrieved a grapefruit and English muffin from the refrigerator, cut both in half, and selected a jar of apricot jelly. Then she sat at the kitchen table to eat. Naturally, she prayed again, thanking God for the food and asking that it would give her the strength she'd been missing.

After breakfast, Marva felt a humble burst of energy, and she picked an apron to wear for as long as her energy would last. She didn't normally wear aprons over her nightgowns or pajamas, but the prospect of wearing one of her favorite aprons and stashing the walkie-talkie in the pocket—just in case—made her smile. The morning's apron read in all caps *YOUR OPINION WASN'T IN THE RECIPE.*

She wandered to the living room and stared a few minutes at a picture of her son, J.R. Then she moved to the mantel and lingered a long time in front of the family Advent calendar. When Marva finally opened the numbered window for December 19, she peeked inside, even though she knew it would be empty.

She turned to face the room and noticed the air around her was lighter just in the few minutes since she'd finished breakfast. Marva's gaze went from one piece of furniture to another, and it seemed the sun was rising quickly, right above her coffee table.

That was fast, she thought. *No, it's too fast,* and the room flashed from bright to white.

She collapsed near the couch.

Marva woke to the sound and sight of EMTs. A blonde woman pulled her eye open and shined a penlight onto her pupil. Another EMT was shouting questions.

"Can you hear me? Do you know where you are? What's your name? Do you know what day it is?"

Marva was just alert enough to be annoyed by the interrogation.

They strapped her to a stretcher and navigated her out the

front door. She saw Zach and Emily standing out of the way on the front porch. Emily had her arm around her son; Marva was too far away to be certain, but it looked as if Zach had been crying.

The elderly porch wavers were away from their guard post, instead standing on the grass near the ambulance and promising Marva they would visit. Marva knew they wouldn't, but she smiled underneath the oxygen mask anyway.

The ambulance raced her to Woodbrook Mercy Hospital, and she was admitted for tests that would last much longer than her energy. Three women from the library visited and snuck in miniature gingerbread cookies they'd made for a holiday luncheon. Her good friend, Rusty Cleveland, visited, too, and spent more time with her than anyone else.

Just before dinner, Emily and Zach stopped by the room for an update. But Marva cut off the small talk with the one question she'd wondered about all day. "How's Charlee?"

Emily took a step closer to the bed and reached for Marva's free hand. "We're here about you, Marva. Any news?"

Marva squeezed Emily's hand firmly. "How's Charlee? Infection better?"

Emily turned her attention from Marva to her son. "Zach, dear, would you go see if your dad is here yet? He said he'd try to be here by dinnertime. Would you check the fourth floor waiting room? If he's not there, ask at the window if he's back with Charlee."

Zach nodded and gave Marva a thumbs-up. She returned

the gesture, and when the door shut behind Zach, Emily slid a chair next to Marva's bed.

Marva pushed a button on the bulky remote and the head of the bed rose until she was in a seated position. "How is she, dear?"

"Not good," Emily half-whispered. "Not good today."

Marva squeezed her hand again. "Fever?"

"Down, but the infection isn't easing up."

Marva sighed a long, painful, "My. I'm sorry."

"It's . . . It's not the way it's supposed to happen, you know?"

"I know, dear."

"The surgery, the treatments have all gone so well. She's been beaten up, tired, you know that happens, though. They tell you all that. What to expect."

Marva wanted to rise up from the bed and hug Emily tight. She looked at the IV and the heart monitor and considered casting it all off.

"She's fighting it, but it's hard, you know? Her system is so weak from the treatments she doesn't have much left to fight the things the rest of us beat all the time. You know?"

Marva nodded because she wanted to comfort her friend, but she also nodded because she knew. She'd seen friends and loved ones seemingly beat the disease itself only to perish from complications of blood clots, the flu, or infections.

Emily pulled her hand away from Marva and took a tissue from a decorative box on the rolling side table.

Marva nodded again. "I'm so sorry, Emily. I'm so sorry this is happening." She ached to say more. She knew there were words for such occasions, but finding them and arranging them in meaningful, comforting order seemed an impossible task with Emily sitting at her side and the distracting hospital hums, beeps, and buzzes filling the air.

They sat without a word until Zach's face appeared in the window. Emily waved him away with a subtle shake of her head.

"Your turn," Emily said, and she pressed both hands against her face as if applying pressure would change the subject.

Marva smiled and checked her pulse on the monitor. "My. Yes, I'm fine. Heart is ticking along."

"What have they told you? You look a little less jaundiced than when they brought you in."

"Could be. They've only decided one thing, really. But it's important."

"And?"

"I'm old."

Emily laughed, and Marva thought it was the most beautiful thing she'd heard all day.

"Seriously, Marva. Nothing yet?"

"They've run scans of everything you can imagine. All the tests you're, quite unfortunately, too familiar with: CAT, MRI, ultrasound, and one called an SRS, I think—it's some sort of injection test."

"Have they ruled anything out?"

Marva narrowed her eyes and lowered her voice. "Only one thing."

Emily's eyes widened, and Marva almost felt guilty about the setup.

"I'm not pregnant."

"Marva Ferguson!" Emily's hands went back to her face, but Marva could tell she was giggling.

"I'm sorry, dear. I couldn't resist."

Marva enjoyed watching Emily compose herself and she wondered how long it had been since her friend had laughed.

"You're too much, Marva. Too much."

Marva let the levity hold them both a moment. "I should know more soon. The doctor said they would gather and consider all the tests and report the results all at once, so as to not worry me."

"Is it working?" Emily asked.

"At my age, there is no worry, there is only waiting."

DECEMBER 19

> *On the 6th Day of Christmas*
> *my true love sent to me:*
> *Six Geese a-Laying*

Dear Charlee:

Please prepare yourself for the touching story of six inspirational geese.

We had traveled to Hawaii in search of the six most perfect geese to present as your Six Geese a-Laying. One day, as we walked the beach collecting seashells, we noticed six colorful geese in a belly dancing class. They were prancing around in their brilliant Hawaiian leis, totally unfazed by the other class members who were laughing and calling them names. Their teasing was so fowl—er, foul!

We watched in awe as they turned the other beak. They returned the taunts with kindness and love. We were impressed! We knew at once that we had found the perfect Six Geese a-Laying.

We promptly scooped them up and began the long trek to our home where they would be allowed to run free until tonight's big delivery.

Great idea, right, Charlee?

Wrong.

We should have known better. The Hawaiian geese did not fare well in the cold. Two days at our home and they all caught the flu. Thankfully, the doctor said they would be fine, but they would never fly again.

What sadness! While we were happy to legally adopt the six geese, what would that mean for the song? For your gift?

Then it hit us. If you couldn't have the geese, you could at least have the leis.

So here you go, Charlee. Please enjoy these six Hawaiian leis. And whenever you sing our song, may you picture our six brave geese running around our backyard a world away. They are the true, original Six Geese a Lei-ing.

Happy 6th Day of Christmas!
The Traveling Elves

DECEMBER 20

> *On the 7th Day of Christmas*
> *my true love sent to me:*
> *Seven Swans a-Swimming*

Dear Charlee:

We're sorry this one came so late in the day. We almost didn't make it! Also, don't think we didn't notice your monkey—what's his name?—watching us from the table in your room. If he learns to talk, we could be in trouble.

All right, let's get back to work!

Years ago our family wrote the seventh verse of our song while touring Russia. The timing was perfect; what better place to find seven live swans a-swimming?

We visited zoos, ponds, and watched every production of Swan Lake we could find. Then one day it occurred to us, we didn't need swans. We needed ducklings! What were we thinking?

So we visited a farm and purchased the seven biggest ducklings we could find. We couldn't have been happier. Sure, the ducklings were ugly, but they'd be swans one day, right?

Feeling quite ducky about our success, we took a day off to enjoy Russia before leaving the country. Plus, the kids had always wanted to tour a bouncy pink rubber ball factory and there was one near our hotel.

We left the seven ducklings on seven duck leashes tied

to the sleigh and bought our tickets. The tour was amazing, and we learned everything you wanted to know about bouncy balls. But the real action started when one of the kids pushed a giant red button marked "Do Not Push!"

Alarms rang out!

Mass panic ensued!

The factory went into meltdown mode!

A sea of hot rubber flowed from the factory!

Everything in sight was coated!

We ran back to the sleigh, and what we saw broke our hearts. Our gaggle of ducklings had been turned into rubber duckies!

It was a stroke of bad duck!

We felt so terrible about what had happened that we just couldn't set them free and start over looking for swans. So the rubber ducks have been with us for every adventure. And, to be honest, we've really grown to love them. They might look different, but we still think they're beautiful. Don't you agree, Charlee?

We've thought of naming them several times, but we knew you'd want the honor. So even though you might not be feeling well this evening, would you please take a minute to name each one?

Charlee, the bad news is they'll never be swans, but the good news is that they don't eat much and they float in the tub.

> Happy 7th Day of Christmas!
> The Traveling Elves

22
Wondering and Wishing

Charlee studied her new, empty room. It wasn't like her room from their old life on Eyring Avenue. It wasn't even her room at the trailer in 27 Homes that she missed more and more every day. But it was a penthouse improvement from the intensive care unit downstairs.

She snuck a glance at Melvin the monkey. He sat on a recliner across the room, tossed aside by a nurse when Charlee made the trip up two floors to her new home at Woodbrook Mercy Hospital. Even Melvin looked ready to go home. She wished she could get out of bed and fetch him, but even with her eyes closed she couldn't picture herself with enough energy to get out of bed on her own. Plus, she didn't want to get in trouble. Charlee thought she'd caused enough trouble already.

She wished she could go home. She thought she felt better,

and she told everyone so. But her mother said the drugs could do that, but only temporarily. The truth was, Charlee still had the infection she'd picked up at home, and she'd overheard the doctor tell her mother it was very serious and very unfortunate, but sadly common in cases like hers. Charlee wished it weren't common in anyone's case.

Charlee hadn't had a fever in twenty-four hours, even though they continued checking with a thermometer every chance they got. She'd asked them to start taking Melvin's temperature too, just for fun, and the nurses downstairs had. But she wasn't sure if the new nurses would be as nice.

Charlee wondered when Miss Marva would call or stop by, especially now that she could have visitors. But Charlee hadn't heard from her for a couple of days, and she missed the sound of her friend's voice. She wished she could talk to her about the mysterious letters and gifts. Was she behind them? If Charlee asked, would Miss Marva pretend not to know but give her a little wink? *It has to be her,* Charlee thought, and it made her love Miss Marva more than ever.

Charlee spotted the white plastic bag with the Woodbrook Mercy Hospital logo on the side. Her treasures. She loved the four stuffed birds she'd gotten, and even from across the room, she could see Big Bird's head smashed against the inside of the bag. She could see the corner of the empty Krispy Kreme box, too, poking above the top of the bag. *I'll save it forever,* she thought, even if she'd already shared the five golden rings with her family on the night the box mysteriously arrived with the silly note.

The six Hawaiian leis hung around her neck, but only because her mother had washed and sanitized each one.

Charlee wondered how long that would be a part of her life. Everyone washed, scrubbed, and sanitized everything before visiting. Zach even had to wear a mask on his last visit because the nurse said she heard a tickle in his throat. Charlee liked that nurse just fine, but the woman didn't understand that Zach's smile was one of the things Charlee liked most about her brother.

Charlee lay down in bed and watched the door. She wondered when it would open. She wished her father would visit. He'd been working again, a lot, and she knew he tried to come by as many times a day as he could. But it wasn't enough.

When would he come? Would he bring a surprise with him? A gift? Better yet, she thought, would he bring a story?

Charlee closed her eyes and wondered when the 8th Day of Christmas would arrive. What would it be? What would the letter say? She began to doze off. What would the gift be?

The opening door startled her. "Hey, sweetheart." Charlee's mother walked in, but she did not let the door close behind her. "Would you like a visitor?"

Charlee slowly sat up. "Who?"

Miss Marva rolled into the room in a wheelchair. Zach was

behind it, carefully pushing, and Charlee thought he was smiling like he had the most important job in the entire hospital.

"Zach! Miss Marva!" Charlee wanted to slide out of bed and hug them, but both her tired body and her mother's eyes said no.

"Hello, sweet Charlee," Miss Marva said. "You look good today."

"I do?"

"My. Of course you do."

"Why are you in a wheelchair?" Before Miss Marva could answer, Charlee noticed Zach poking his head into the hospital bag of gifts. "Did you see what I got, Zach?"

He began to answer, but Emily interrupted them both and asked Zach to wait outside. "There will be time for that later, kids. Miss Marva can't stay long, and she wants to visit with Charlee."

Zach complied with a grouchy shrug.

"Charlee, Miss Marva wants to stay a minute. Are you up for it?"

"Yes! I love visitors, especially Miss Marva's kind." Charlee giggled at herself, but didn't know why. She only knew she was excited to see her best friend.

"I'll be right outside," Emily said. Then she pushed Miss Marva closer to Charlee's bed. "You sure you don't want me to stay?"

Miss Marva's eyes must have said no, because even though

Charlee didn't hear anything, her mother quietly stepped out-side.

"I'm so glad you're here," Charlee said to her friend. "Are your legs hurting?"

"A bit."

"Are you feeling slow today?"

"Well, yes, I guess I am. I'm feeling very slow today. That's a good way of putting it."

"I'm sorry," Charlee said and then squeaked, "Oh! Guess what?"

Miss Marva smiled. "What?"

"Dad got his own apron from Mr. Rusty."

"I heard."

"Dad said he brought it to our house. He promised to wear it for me."

"He did?"

"I don't remember what it said though. Do you?"

Miss Marva hesitated. "I sure do. It had a quote from a writer."

"A quote?"

"Like when someone says something really important."

"Oh."

"It's actually one of my favorite quotes from one of my favorite writers. Have you heard of C. S. Lewis?"

"I don't think so."

"Well, if God has His way, you will. The apron says *Reason is the natural order of truth; but imagination is the organ of meaning."*

"That's nice," she breathed. "What does it mean?"

"It means stories are really, really important."

Charlee pictured her dad wearing it and said, "I hope Dad wears it a lot."

Miss Marva agreed and let the silence hang before continuing. "So, Charlee, I need to talk to you about my wheelchair."

"Have you talked to a doctor? I have one you could talk to."

Miss Marva smiled and shifted in her chair. Then she rolled herself a little closer to Charlee's bed. "That's why I'm here, Charlee. I've been talking to doctors for a few days now."

Charlee instantly felt at least five more questions rise to her tongue, but she held her breath and let Miss Marva continue.

"I'm sick, Charlee. I have been for a while, they think, and it's a little bit like what you've had."

"Cancer?"

Marva looked away and out the window into the hallway a moment before turning back and connecting with Charlee's eyes. "Yes, Charlee. Cancer."

"Is it a tumor? Like mine? It's gone, they said."

"I know, and that's the greatest news ever. But it's not quite like yours, no. Mine is bigger, and more spread out."

"Where?"

"Well, it's in my pancreas. Have you heard of that?"

Charlee shook her head.

"It's by my stomach. Right next door."

"In the same neighborhood," Charlee offered more as an observation than a question. "The way we're neighbors."

"That's right."

Charlee remained quiet, studying Miss Marva's face, hospital gown, and unusually messy hair. "So they'll take it out, like they did mine, and you'll go home."

"I wish they could, sweetheart, but it's not that easy in my case."

"Why not?"

"I think because . . . I think it's bigger than yours."

"The tumor?"

"That's right. It's much bigger than the one they removed from you."

"Can they make two trips?"

Marva smiled, but Charlee noticed that her laugh didn't follow the way it always had.

"I'm afraid not, Charlee. Mine is the kind that starts in one place, but grows to lots of others. No matter how much you want it to stop, it just grows until it's in a lot of places."

"Like weeds," Charlee said. And her mind went from her drab hospital room to the green and yellow field between the edge of Miss Marva's yard and her own. Charlee looked at Miss Marva's blotchy hands and ran her small fingers over the mud-pie colored patches.

"You're very, very bright, Charlee Alexander. Yes, like weeds. It's growing in me like weeds that can't be pulled or killed. There are just too many in the field, and they've been growing for a long time. We just didn't know it."

Charlee noticed her mother standing just outside the door looking in through the small window, and even from across the room, she could see her mother's cheeks were wet. She looked back at Miss Marva to find her cheeks were wet, too.

"Are you going to die, Miss Marva?"

When she didn't answer right away, Charlee used the silence to pull a tissue from the box on the side table and press it against Marva's cheek. She asked again, "Are you going to die?"

Miss Marva breathed in deeply but did not look away. "Yes."

The word brought tears to Charlee's tired eyes and soon her cheeks were wet, too. She lay her head down and let the tears run down her nose to her lips and chin. "Miss Marva?"

"Yes, dear."

"Am I going to die, too?"

DECEMBER 21

On the 8th Day of Christmas
my true love sent to me:
Eight Maids a-Milking

Dear Charlee:

We know you might be feeling extra sick right now, but we're thinking of you, and we hope you can't wait each day for your next verse and gift. We love sharing them with you!

Okay, are you sitting down for this one? You better be because this story is pretty amazing.

We'd been working hard for a long time when we woke up one day and realized we needed a vacation. We debated for a long time about where to go. Disneyland? The mountains? Mars? There were so many options.

Then the kids suggested London, England. Of course! We checked into a hotel and had a wonderful week seeing the sights. Every night we'd come back to the hotel and couldn't believe what an amazing job the maids had done.

No matter how messy we were, they always made the room look brand-new and spotless. They were the hardest-working maids we'd ever seen.

We were so impressed with these eight talented maids that we decided to write them into the song. The verse was meant to be, "On the 8th Day of Christmas, my true love gave to me, eight maids a-cleaning." We sang it all the time.

When the day arrived to check out of the hotel, we made them an offer they couldn't refuse. We would show them the world if they would serve as our official Eight Maids in the song.

They agreed!

We put the maids in the sleigh and headed out of town.

Here comes the good news and bad news. The good news is that we picked up a cow in Nebraska to save money on milk. (You wouldn't believe how much milk the kids go through!)

The bad news is that we sat the maids and the cow next to each other in the sleigh. Wouldn't you know it, those Eight Maids got right to work and milked for so long and so sweetly that the cows started to make caramels instead of milk! It wasn't a miracle—it was a milkacle!

We had no choice but to change the song.

So tonight you get eight Milk Maid Caramels. They won't do much cleaning, or milking for that matter, but they sure taste good if you unwrap and eat them.

Happy 8th Day of Christmas!
The Traveling Elves

23
Neighbors

Marva made her pitch to every nurse, doctor, and janitor who would listen. There was no reason she couldn't move to the pediatric wing and be closer to Charlee, and she didn't care how unusual the request was.

"You can move me, or I can move myself," she told the chief oncologist. "I've been up there, and I know there's at least one empty room." When the doctor hesitated, she narrowed her eyes and said, "Put me in it."

He did.

Later, when Marva was settled across the hall from Charlee in a room with clouds on the ceiling and ponies on the wall, she sent for the doctor and apologized for her brashness.

On her first day as Charlee's neighbor at Woodbrook Mercy Hospital, despite feeling more fatigued than she had the day she collapsed at home, Marva insisted on lunch in Charlee's room. The nurse obliged, but only on the conditions that Marva wear a mask when she wasn't eating and that Charlee's parents agreed to the idea.

They did, and an attendant rolled Marva into Charlee's room.

"Have lunch with me today?" Marva asked.

"Uh-huh."

"How are you?"

"Tired."

"Me, too. You're not eating today, Charlee?"

Charlee pointed to her IV bag.

"I see."

Marva slumped slightly in her chair and watched her frail friend clutch Melvin and drift in and out. "How about I do most of the talking today?"

Charlee nodded.

"All right. Let's see . . ." Marva surveyed the room. "Did you get your 12 Days gift today yet?"

Charlee shook her head, no.

"What day of Christmas is it? The 8th? The 9th?"

Charlee nodded.

"Do you know yet who your elf friends are?"

Charlee lifted Melvin's finger and pointed at Marva.

"Nope, I'm not writing those letters, Charlee. It's not me."

Marva couldn't tell if Charlee looked confused, disappointed, or simply too hazy-eyed from the medication. "Let's see, day nine is the ladies dancing, right? I wonder what's coming." Marva wanted to smile, but was deeply discouraged at how much energy it took to even finish a sentence. "I should come back."

Charlee shook her head again.

"But you look so tired today, Charlee."

No response.

"Truth is, I'm tired too. More tests . . . More doctors . . . More of everything." Marva took a beat. "Oh, Charlee, I wish I could be as brave as you've been. I just don't know how you've done it. . . . You're quite a courageous young lady, you know that?"

Charlee's mouth grew into a half-grin that threatened to become a full smile.

"It's true, Charlee, you've just been so brave. So. Brave."

Then came the wide smile.

"There's the smile. . . . Now, do you know what you want for Christmas?"

Charlee's smile softened. "Uh-huh."

"What?"

"I want us to be home for Christmas."

"My. Surely you want something else, too?"

Charlee hesitated and closed her eyes before opening them halfway. "Mostly that," she whispered.

Marva watched Charlee drift off to sleep. During her short nap, and despite having no appetite, she ate a cup of raspberry gelatin and a piece of wheat toast to avoid the crusty looks she'd get from her own team of nurses.

Marva valiantly fought the blue visions of sad memories, but as Charlee slept, she couldn't avoid seeing again the final moments of her husband's life. She'd been there in his room for the death rattle. She'd been there when, on three separate occasions, John had called out the names of loved ones who'd already passed on, as if waiting for one of them to escort him across a bridge only they could see. Marva had been there when the race slowed to a peaceful march and then, finally, to a quiet tiptoe home to heaven.

Marva had thought of John as perpetually young. But at fifty years old, he was a veteran of marriage and fatherhood and a career. He'd lived through everything cancer was threatening to keep from Charlee.

The thought made Marva angry, and whatever appetite she had left for cold toast and warm gelatin vanished. She pulled her mask over her mouth and took a deep breath. She looked at Charlee's IV and considered her infection a prison, blocking a full, happy life out of spite and nothing more. There was no just cause, no rightful reason except randomness and the statistics that refused to lie. The feeling made Marva nauseous.

Marva imagined a funeral for the little girl; then she erased the picture. She saw 27 Homes without Charlee trying to befriend ornery neighbors or porch wavers; then she swallowed those thoughts like painful horse pills.

She closed her eyes and saw her son, J.R., on a field she

never actually saw, in a country she never visited in person, in a war she never understood. He was young, bleeding, and sending his last letter home on the only piece of paper he could find.

Marva leaned forward and stroked Charlee's pale arm. For the first time since Black Friday, Marva realized that she'd lost her best friend not once, but twice.

Charlee would make three.

DECEMBER 22

On the 9th Day of Christmas
my true love sent to me:
Nine Ladies Dancing

Dear Charlee:

This is a heart-wrenching story, but if you are pa-tient—in the end—you will be blessed with a story of faith, hope, and perseverance.

It all started in 1954. Walt Disney was making prep-arations for the release of Lady and the Tramp. Have you seen it?

The animation was complete and casting had begun for the part of Lady. Dogs from all over California were summoned to an audition in LA by canine super-agent Harry Schnauzer. (Side note: Schnauzer went on to repre-sent Lassie, Benji, ALF, and the alien from E.T.)

The mood was tense as one by one the dogs sang and danced for the team of directors and producers. One lucky pooch was on the verge of fame and fortune, and eight other dogs would be cast in supporting roles.

It came down to ten finalists and a dancing competi-tion to determine who would play the part opposite the Tramp and who would earn the smaller roles.

The competition was fierce. Hair flew and drool puddled in all corners of the dance studio. Panting could be heard as far away as San Diego!

But in the end, one dog came through as the clear choice. She was cast on the spot and would become a leading lady legend. Eight others were cast. But one—just one—was sent home empty-pawed.

Her dreams were dashed.

In a quirk of fate, on this same afternoon, the family and I were walking down Rodeo Drive. We rounded a corner to find this one puppy, this one wannabe Lady, sitting on the curb watching the cars dash by. We offered to buy her a cupcake and listen to her woes.

Then came the miracle. My dear sensitive wife, in a stroke of genius, explained that we were casting our own project and needed a dancing Lady of our own. We asked, "Would you like to join us?"

She barked, "Yes!"

We sang the ninth verse of our song for her and she loved it! Even more, she was honored to represent all nine ladies dancing.

So tonight, we present you with this stuffed pooch— the finest lady ever—the one who represents all nine!

Happy 9th Day of Christmas!
The Traveling Elves

24
Talkies, but Not Walkies

Charlee felt more awake than she had in days. She picked up the phone by her bed and dialed Miss Marva's room across the hall.

"Hello?"

"Is this Miss Marva?"

"Speaking. Is this Zach?"

"No." Charlee giggled.

"Oh, Mr. Alexander?"

"No!"

"Emily?"

"Warmer!"

"Then it can only be . . ."

"Yes?"

"Melvin, how are you?"

"Colder, colder! It's Charlee. You knew it was me, didn't you?"

"My. I suppose I did. Yes. And don't you sound chipper today."

"I do?"

"You sure do."

"Do you feel chipper today, Miss Marva? I thought you were going to visit me today."

"I was, sweetheart, but the doctor said I'm too weak to leave my room today. I'm not quite as chipper as you, I guess."

"I'm sorry."

"My. Don't be sorry. It's all right. I'll be just fine."

Charlee switched the phone to her other ear and rolled over in bed so she was facing Marva's room. "I miss our walkie-talkies."

"Me too. Those were fun, weren't they?"

"Yeah. The phone isn't as fun. Plus we can't really walk."

"But we can still talk, right, Charlee?"

"Yeah. I guess they're talkies, but not walkies."

Charlee heard Miss Marva laugh through the phone, and even though she couldn't see the matching smile, the sound made her happy.

"Guess who visited me today?" Miss Marva asked.

"Who?"

"Zach."

"He did?"

"Yes, he came over after he left your room with your mom."

"That was nice."

"It sure was. He visits me a lot, you know."

"He does?"

"Sure. He's even been running errands for me, like my own messenger. He's brought me some things from home and checked my mail. He's been very helpful and one of my very best visitors."

"That's nice. He visits me a lot, too."

"Well, of course he does, Charlee, he loves you. You know how much he loves you?"

"I think so."

"He does. Even when he visits me, all he talks about is you."

Charlee smiled. "I had another visitor, too. Nurse Becky. She was my nurse before—after my operation—but she still checks on me even though she said I'm not in her department anymore."

"My. That's so sweet."

"Uh-huh. She said she told her bosses that she wanted to still work with me, and they said I could still be one of hers, even if I wasn't like an official patient."

"She sounds nice. I'd like to meet her sometime." The line went silent before Marva continued. "Where's your mom right now, sweetheart?"

"She went with my dad to talk to the doctor a while ago."

"That's good. Your dad isn't working today?"

"No, his new work said he didn't have to come back until after January and that he could call first."

Charlee wondered why Miss Marva took so long to reply. "Are you there?"

"Yes, I'm sorry. I'm here. I'm just so happy that you sound better today. You sound like your old Charlee."

"Mom says I slept good last night and that helps me feel better."

"She's right, as always."

Charlee took a sip of juice from her leftover lunch. "Guess what?"

"What?"

"I got a cute stuffed puppy dog for the 9th Day of Christmas."

"A puppy?" Miss Marva said. "I thought it was ladies dancing?"

"It is." Charlee snickered. "I'll show you the letter when you visit me."

"My. Now I'll have to come see you."

"Yep."

The two friends stayed quiet a moment, and Charlee wondered just how long it would be until Marva was able to come back across the hall, but she decided not to bother her with asking. Plus, she didn't want to jinx their luck. It had been bad enough already.

"I'm glad you're enjoying the Days of Christmas so much, Charlee. Someone must really love you."

"Do you think I'll ever find out who the elves are?"

"I don't know, sweetheart. I suppose if it's meant to be, you will. But sometimes keeping things like this a secret is part of the fun."

"Yeah."

After another moment, Miss Marva said, "Did I tell you that my friend, Rusty, visited me last night? He brought me an apron as an early Christmas gift."

"What does it say?"

"It says, *I can only please one person a day. Today is not your day, and tomorrow doesn't look good either.*"

"But that's not true, Miss Marva. You please a lot of people every day."

Miss Marva laughed again, but this time it was loud enough that Charlee didn't need the phone to hear the giggles, she could hear her from across the hall. Normally, Miss Marva's laughter was like the best medicine Charlee had ever tried. But this time, having it so close but still separated by all those stupid bricks, it actually made her lonelier and sadder. She'd give anything to be sitting next to Miss Marva, or hanging laundry with her, or rearranging her apron collection.

She'd even be happy, she thought, to stand on the stump in the backyard of their trailer and be separated by the field she loved so much. Just to see Miss Marva in her yard, even from a distance, would be so much nicer than listening to her scratchy, sick voice on the ugly hospital telephone.

"Miss Marva?"

"Yes?"

"I want to go home for Christmas."

"I know you do, Charlee."

"Do you want to be home for Christmas?"

"My. Yes, very much, Charlee."

"Miss Marva?"

"Yes?"

"If only one of us can be home. I hope it's you."

DECEMBER 23

On the 10th Day of Christmas
my true love sent to me:
Ten Lords a-Leaping

Dear Charlee:

Our helpers tell us you're still fighting hard. Please don't stop. Please don't give up, Charlee. We need you. We need you to finish the 13 Days of Christmas with us. After that, we need you to finish many, many days and live many, many more dreams.

Keep fighting!

This is Day Ten, and it's one of our favorites!

The year was 1779. We were celebrating New Year's Eve with the famous Dick Clark in Times Square. The crowd was having a grand time, firing their muskets into the air and dancing around the wagons. Everything was perfect, until . . .

At exactly 11:50 P.M., the famous Flying Mozart paratroopers were supposed to drop from the sky and make a slow descent into Times Square. But Dick had forgotten to send the appearance fee, and they were all the way in Los Angeles at a grand opening for a new piano store!

What would he do?

In a jolt of inspiration, he picked up his cell phone and called his good friend King George III.

"George, I need you!" Dick said.

"Anything for you," replied the king.

Dick explained his dilemma and the missing Flying Mozart parachuting act.

"Stand by," said the king. "Help is on the way."

A roar was soon heard overhead. Every eye looked heavenward and lo and behold, from high in the sky, we saw ten men, one after another, leaping from an early prototype Zeppelin airship.

You guessed it! King George had sent ten men from his House of Lords to entertain the guests gathered in Times Square. That gesture—though rarely mentioned in history books—is one of the reasons the war would eventually come to an end. Yes, Charlee, it's true. There were no tears that night; we celebrated the New Year with the king's own Ten Lords a-Leaping!

We had no choice but to immediately invite them to serve as your gift for tonight. They couldn't come personally, of course, because of their commitments in England, but they sent along these ten plastic parachuting toy men to remember them by.

Happy 10th Day of Christmas!
The Traveling Elves

25
Mason

Thomas and Zach rode up in the elevator in silence. Zach carried Marva's house key and a bag of things she'd requested from her home. Thomas carried only the heavy rocks of debt and worry.

Thomas watched the lights in the elevator announce each passing floor. They seemed to move slower than the elevator, as if unsure of where they were headed. Thomas had spent the day negotiating with the health insurance company they'd used back in their old life when both his business and his daughter were healthy on Eyring Avenue.

He'd kept the policy when they lost the home to foreclosure and a bad mortgage and the business to his own decisions and a bad economy. But he'd missed a few payments since they'd picked up the pieces and moved, and a heated debate was brewing over when the coverage lapsed, what the provider would pay, and what bills the Alexanders would at least promise to pay, but would likely have to hide from for years.

The relentless second-guessing was such a present part of Thomas's daily routine that he didn't know what it felt like to live confidently anymore.

I'm out of first guesses, he thought. *So why bother?*

The weight of losing their home and business, of seeing Zach embarrassed and laughed out of school, was a pack of rocks too heavy to carry. But that was nothing compared to the unfair weight of watching his daughter play on death's teeter-totter while simultaneously worrying which bill collector's number would hit the caller ID next. They'd escaped to Woodbrook for a fresh start and to lighten their burdens, but they'd settled into a life of less freedom and greater challenges than they'd ever known or asked for.

The elevator beeped and bounced to a stop, and they stepped out onto the sixth floor of Woodbrook Mercy Hospital and took the familiar path to Charlee's room. They found Emily sitting on the side of Charlee's bed, reading a book.

"Look who's here," Emily said through her mask, as Thomas and Zach appeared at the door. "Masks, boys," she said, pointing to a disposable box of them hanging on the wall just inside the door. They put their own on and exchanged quick hellos, but then Emily and Zach eased out to visit Marva so Thomas and Charlee could have a few minutes of one-on-one time.

"What do you think?" Thomas asked as he straightened the apron with the C. S. Lewis quote on it so Charlee could read it. The fabric was snug over his winter coat.

"I really, really, really love it."

Thomas grinned. "Three *really*s?"

"Really," she added. "And I know what it means."

"You do?"

"It means stories are important."

Thomas nodded and settled into the warm impression Emily left at Charlee's side in the bed. Thomas noted that even with him in it, the bed seemed to swallow them.

"Hi, there," he said. "What's your name?"

"Charlee."

"Nice to meet you. I'm Thomas Alexander."

Charlee tried to narrow her eyes, and Thomas wondered if she was trying to imitate one of her mother's looks. "You look familiar, mister."

The two chatted about Charlee's day and her growing concern that Christmas would come and go and she would still be in the hospital. Thomas reminded her it wasn't exactly their decision to make, but that they hadn't given up hope.

Charlee asked her father about the neighborhood and whether anyone had asked about her. She wondered if he'd been by to greet the porch wavers, or say hello to the kids at the rock pile on the short dead-end street they called the barb in their fishhook-shaped neighborhood.

He hadn't, he said, but only because he'd been too worried about her to do much else.

Charlee asked about the VW Beetle in the yard and wanted to know if they'd tried driving it around 27 Homes yet.

They had, he said, and Zach had even tried driving it up and down the long shank road.

"Zach's driving? Cool!"

"Not exactly. He's sort of driving; he's not technically old enough yet, but he's pretty good. I didn't think anyone would mind if he practiced in the neighborhood. Plus, I was sitting next to him."

"Was Mom in the backseat? Mom hates the backseat."

"Also not exactly," Thomas said, and he pivoted the discussion to something else; he didn't want to risk a line of questioning from Emily later. "I heard you got some parachute men today."

"I did! They're right there." Charlee pointed at the chair in the corner. I was playing with them earlier, but Mom didn't want me to try them in here."

"Why not?"

"Not safe, she said."

"Not safe? Let's see about that." Thomas edged off the bed and retrieved one of the small plastic men from the chair. He removed the small rubber band securing the parachute to the man's back and surveyed the room for options. He stepped into the bathroom and almost immediately poked his head back into the room. "I've got an idea."

Charlee answered with wide eyes.

Thomas wiggled his eyebrows in mischief and disappeared back into the bathroom. When he reappeared, he was carrying a small hospital hair dryer he'd unplugged from the wall. The irony of a bald girl having a hair dryer in her bathroom was not lost on him then or later, when he shared the experience with Zach and Emily.

Thomas plugged the hair dryer into an outlet by Charlee's bed and set the temperature to cool and the fan to low. Then he tossed the paratrooper into the air and aimed the dryer up, sending the man flying across the room and bouncing off a wall-mounted whiteboard the nurses used for messages to and from each other. Thomas couldn't tell if Charlee was smiling, because she had both hands covering her mouth in surprise, but her eyes had the same wide and curious expression as before. "Let's try that again, shall we?"

Charlee nodded with gusto.

It took several efforts, but eventually Thomas thought to position the hair dryer blowing upward first, then carefully place the paratrooper over the airflow with his hand supporting the chute from above until it was steady. When he finally removed his hand, the Lord a-Leaping hovered in the air eighteen inches above the hair dryer.

"That's amazing!" Charlee squealed. She convinced her father to try two, then three, of the men at once, but they found the arrangement could only support one at a time.

The fun ended when a nurse came to check Charlee's

vitals. She plucked the paratrooper from the air and placed it in Charlee's lap. "You have to be licensed for that kind of flying at Woodbrook Mercy," she said with a wink.

Thomas returned the hair dryer to the bathroom while the nurse recorded Charlee's pulse, blood pressure, and several readings from the IV into a handheld computer. When she said good-bye, Thomas nestled back into the spot next to his daughter. He playfully tugged Melvin from Charlee's firm grip. "Hi, there, you look familiar, too. What's your name again? Moleson? Koleson? No, wait, Jason? Kason? Mason?"

"It's Melvin, Dad."

"It is? It's not Mason? From our stories?"

"I changed it, remember? He wanted a fresh start, too."

Thomas was sure he'd heard that, but in that moment, he was embarrassed. Charlee must have recognized it, he realized, because she quickly said, "You've been really busy, Daddy. It's all right. I bet Melvin doesn't remember your name either." Her sweet attempt to save him embarrassed Thomas even more.

"You remember our stories?" Thomas asked.

"Sure, Dad. It hasn't been that long. I miss them." She reached over and lifted Melvin's long arm. "So does Melvin."

Thomas raised Melvin's other arm. "How about one tonight?"

"Right here?" Charlee asked.

"Sure."

"Right now? With your mask on?"

"Absolutely. It makes me mysteeeeerious." Thomas looked

around the room, pretending to make sure they were alone. "Ready?"

Charlee nodded and snuggled closer to her father. The warmth distracted him for a moment, and it seemed to Thomas that neither rushed to break the silence.

"Once upon a time, there was a very happy monkey in a big house in a big town like the one we used to live in."

"Woodbrook?"

"Oh, no. Someplace better, like our old neighborhood. His name was Melvin, and he'd just learned a big challenge was ahead for him and his family. He was about to go on a wild, scary adventure—"

"Dad?" Charlee interrupted.

"Uh-huh?"

"You don't need to do that anymore."

Thomas knew what she meant, and he wondered what else she'd learned and how far she had moved along while he was distracted by his life's bag of heavy rocks.

"No stories from before?"

"No. He wants a new one, and I'd like a new one, too. Something brand-brand-new."

"Brand-brand?"

Charlee and Melvin nodded.

"All right. Once upon a time there was a monkey named Melvin. But he wasn't an ordinary monkey, he was also secretly a race car driver."

"Really?"

"Yes, really, and he drives a Beetle. Can you believe it?"

Thomas wove an intricate story that took father, daughter, and monkey on an unbelievable adventure far from Woodbrook Mercy Hospital. Soon they forgot why they were there, or that Charlee was still deep in disease woods, or that Christmas was knocking on their doorstep.

In fact, soon they were so deep in the story, they didn't even realize that Zach and Emily had joined them for the ride.

DECEMBER 24

> *On the 11th Day of Christmas*
> *my true love sent to me:*
> *Eleven Pipers Piping*

Dear Charlee:

Can you believe we're almost done? It seems like just yesterday we made our first delivery. Now Christmas is just a day away. Are you hanging in there?

The story of the Eleven Pipers Piping started many years ago while we were watching the Macy's Thanksgiving Day Parade live and in person! It had always been our dream, and it was finally coming true.

We were sitting on the parade route and coming up with ideas for Day Eleven. Every new float, band, or balloon gave us another idea.

"What about the 11 Snoopys Snooping?"

"Wait! What about the 11 Lip-Synchers Syncing?"

"I got it! The 11 Matt Lauers Looking Lovely!"

There was no shortage of ideas, but a definite lack of good ones.

We had almost given up hope when the final marching band of the day came down the parade route. It featured eleven men playing patriotic music on kazoos. The music was beautiful!

We kept pace with them and were waiting for them when the parade ended. We explained the song, the new verse they inspired, and our special mission. Before we could even ask, they'd offered to donate their kazoos to you, Charlee, as part of this special night.

They promised us that if they could have come in person tonight to Woodbrook, they would have. But they were already committed to another gig in Atlantic City.

But don't be discouraged! They guaranteed that their pipes—I mean kazoos—would be easy to learn to play and you'd soon be joining in parades, too.

So get better, Charlee, and get practicing! The world needs your kazoo talent!

Happy 11th Day of Christmas!
The Traveling Elves

26
Christmas Eve

Can I stay? Please?" Zach pled.

Zach watched his parents exchange those serious adult looks that say everything in silence. He usually avoided those looks, preferring to roll his eyes and tune back in when they were done talking about him—or in this case, looking about him.

"Nurse?" Thomas said.

She looked at Zach, and he was encouraged by her smile. "It's your decision, Mr. Alexander. But I'd say, Why not?"

Thomas put his hand on Zach's shoulder and winked. It was the first time since moving to Woodbrook that Zach felt trusted. *No,* he thought, *it's more than that.* He felt like a man.

Nurse Becky smiled again before becoming serious and opening a red hospital file folder. "Close in," she said, and the four of them tightened their circle in the hallway outside Charlee's door. "I've spoken with the team, and they're willing to sign off on this."

Emily clapped her hands together and held them in a prayer pose.

"Sweet," Zach said.

Thomas nodded and kept nodding as Nurse Becky continued.

"But you need to know the risks. All right?"

Three heads nodded in unison.

"The infection is retreating. It's so much better, but she's still at risk. She simply does not have the ability to fight the kinds of bugs and viruses that healthy people like us fend off every day. Her immune system remains weak."

"But it's normal, right?" Emily said. "Everyone has been saying the treatments would do that."

"Correct. It happens as part of the process. The fatigue and susceptibility to other, unrelated sickness is completely normal. But it does mean that we have to be much more careful. You don't want her back here with a fever again."

"Of course not," Thomas said.

"So when can we leave?" Emily asked, getting the discussion back to the question they'd been asking for days.

"Soon. We want to get numbers one more time, and then it will take a little while to get the paperwork generated." Nurse Becky closed the folder and held it against her chest with her arms crossed. "Listen, no guests. No trips outside the house.

Lots of liquids—water, water, water. And calories are Charlee's friend."

"Really?"

"Yes, and not just her friend, but her best friend. She needs calories, and it doesn't matter how she gets them. Liquids are good, of course. Gatorade, but not the low-cal kind. Candy, cookies, whatever."

"So all the things we're usually supposed to say no to," Emily said.

"Exactly. Of course healthy foods are best, but she needs the calories, the energy. You must have a house full of Christmas goodies. So say yes to just about everything. Bake cookies together and let her eat the frosting straight from the little tub."

"You know, Mom," Zach said, scratching his chin, "I've been pretty tired lately, too."

The laughter filled the hallway and made Zach stand taller than usual.

"Also, be sure Charlee gets plenty of sleep. She'll wear down very easily. She should head to bed before she says she's tired. If she's complaining about being tired or having a headache, you waited too long to shut her down for the day."

Emily started to ask another question but Nurse Becky cut her off with a raised index finger. "She'll be excited to be home. Now, multiply that by the fact that it's Christmas Eve, and the fact that she's a child. She's going to need to be reeled in."

Emily tried again and the finger went back up.

Zach stifled a snicker.

"If her fever hits 100 flat, you're back here. Don't call and ask, all right? Bundle her up and get here." She looked at Emily and let the tension go from her face. "Okay, now you're up."

"Sorry about that. I'm just anxious."

"We're all anxious," Thomas said, and Zach nodded thoughtfully the way he thought any adult would in that situation.

"When do we come back?" Emily finally asked.

"Hopefully we don't see you again until the 27th. Tuesday. Sound good to everyone? If she's still improving, she'll go right back home with you and we'll get the treatments restarted. But again, the doctor wants her back before then if the fever runs high, or if you see any other warning signs. You can't be too careful."

Emily said thank you and gave Nurse Becky a hug. Then she said thank you again before letting go.

Thomas also thanked Nurse Becky and gave her a two-handed handshake.

Zach did the same, even though he thought she deserved a million hugs for helping Charlee get home for Christmas.

Zach and his parents shared the good news with Charlee, and by the time they'd finished, she was already gathering up her eleven kazoos into the gift bag. Zach's mother laid out the conditions of her return home for the holiday and Charlee agreed before hearing them all.

"Wait," Charlee said, interrupting her mother's lecture. "What about Miss Marva? Is she going home, too?"

Thomas and Emily did the look thing again, and this time Zach looked away because he already knew the sad answer.

"I don't think so," Emily said. "She's just not up for it."

"No, not yet, Charlee Chew," Thomas added, "but she will be. She just needs more strength."

Charlee looked at Zach and, in her tears, he was sure he saw the enthusiasm flow past him and right under the door like spilled water.

"That's not fair," Charlee said. "That's all I wanted for Christmas. For both of us to be home. It's. Not. Fair."

"I know it's not," Emily said, sitting on the edge of the bed and pulling her daughter into a side-hug. "But you can say good-bye on your way out, how about that? And you can call her tomorrow."

"Or even tonight before bed," Thomas added. "If you'd like to."

Charlee sniffled, and her mother turned to Zach. "Son, would you step across the hall and see if Marva is awake? Tell her she has a special visitor."

"Yep," he said, and he spun on a heel to leave the room. He took three big steps and pushed Marva's door open. "Miss Marva? Are you up?"

"Come in," she said softly. "You're just the man I was looking for."

27
Home

For the first time in weeks, Marva's insomnia wasn't caused by pain, discomfort, or loneliness. It was the unmistakable feeling of hope that kept her up all night long. She had hope for the morning, she had hope for Christmas Day and all it meant to her, and, like every other year, she hoped to wake up on December 26 a better person.

She looked at the clock on the wall: 4:45 A.M. She checked the time on the cheap digital watch she'd worn all night: 4:45 A.M. *It's time,* she thought. Given how slowly she was moving these days, and how her dull, constant back pain had been replaced by fire, she calculated that the extra time was a must.

Marva slid her legs around and off the bed like two heavy pieces of furniture. She left the IV in her wrist but removed the oxygen tubes from her nose so she'd have less to pull down the hallway. She pulled on a pair of thick flannel pajama bottoms, slid her feet into fur-lined moccasins, and pushed open the door to peek out. Two nurses gabbed inside the glass-enclosed nurses' station, which was adorned with tinsel and twinkling lights.

Marva shuffled down the hallway a foot at a time, appearing to admire the decorations and children's holiday drawings that lined her path like wallpaper. She stopped at one with Charlee's name scrawled across the top. It was, quite clearly, a view of 27 Homes from above. Charlee had drawn the fishhook shape and small boxes to represent every trailer, each one connected to the crayon roads by a black dash.

Charlee's trailer had four stick figures inside. A green field ran behind it to a much larger home with a clothesline to its left. An oversized stick figure in a striped dress stood next to the house, standing as tall as the roofline. But Marva looked closer and realized the dress wasn't a dress at all; it was an apron. She stepped even closer and saw that it read *Dorothy was right. There's no place like home.*

Marva would have laughed if her sides hadn't ached, so instead she smiled and pulled the drawing from the wall, leaving four loops of tape stuck awkwardly to the shiny paint. She folded the construction paper and stuck it in the pocket of her hospital gown.

Marva moved on, willing the squeaky wheels of her IV cart to remain quiet as she snuck down the hallway. She approached the nurses' station and took a long breath as the two chatty women passed in her peripheral vision. The elevator was around the corner, just past a display of glossy framed head-shots of Woodbrook Mercy Hospital's many distinguished administrators. Marva judged that only fifteen steps separated her from the down button.

"Ms. Ferguson?"

Marva might have cursed if she had the energy.

"Are you all right? What are you doing out of bed?" One of the nurses approached with her hands on her hips.

"My. I'm just fine. I needed to stretch my legs, that's all."

"Ms. Ferguson, it's the middle of the night."

"Precisely," Marva said. "Just when they need some stretching. I couldn't lie down anymore, I'm sorry. I hadn't been up, not even for a moment, all day yesterday. I really needed to be up a bit. Just for a bit. The doctor said if I could, I should."

The nurse examined Marva's IV bag, flicked the tube, and put her hands back on her hips. When she started to speak again, Marva cut her off by tapping one of the photos on the wall with her index finger. "This one's cute."

The nurse chuckled. "He might be too young for both of us, I'm afraid."

"Nonsense. I might look old and all used up, but I'm young at heart."

"Well, that's certainly true."

"My. I suspect that gentleman couldn't keep up with me on the dance floor. I had some moves in my day—bet I still do."

Marva tried to shake her hips side to side, and a shot of pain ran like a hot bullet up her spine.

The nurse laughed again and relaxed her hands from her hips, dropping them into the pockets of her blue scrubs. Marva quickly found another talking point. "Look at these two side-by-side. Austin Westover and Mitra Westover. Related?"

"Married," the nurse said. "Met in college, I hear, and inseparable. He married way outside of his league, if you ask me. She's beautiful, and he's just so, so, goofy-looking." The nurse stepped closer to the wall as if to confirm her opinion and examine the photos more closely. "Want to know a secret?"

"Do clothes dry on a line?"

"That one there"—the nurse pointed to a different doctor—"I went to high school with him."

Marva leaned in close to read the name. "Dr. Michael Mandel?"

"He was so cute back then. Even went on a date with him once. But look at him now. I can't tell which chin came first."

Marva couldn't contain the laughter, and though it took nearly everything she had in the tank, she howled as best she could for an eighty-one-year-old woman riddled with cancer. "You're just awful," Marva said, when she finally caught her breath.

They admired a few other photos together until the nurse was called to assist in another patient's room. "I'll be right back, then it's off to bed for you, all right? Just one minute."

The nurse scampered off, and Marva waited until she'd

disappeared into a room. Then she pressed forward, rounded the corner, and hit the elevator's down button. Less than ten seconds later, she was smiling as the doors closed.

The doors reopened on the main level, and a janitor passed by, sloshing a mop bucket. "Merry Christmas," he said, and Marva returned the greeting with another smile and a nod.

She deliberately walked away from the bay of four elevators and into the atrium near the lobby. Bing Crosby played lightly through the overhead speakers, and the biggest Christmas tree she'd ever seen stood proudly in the middle of the room, surrounded by a velvet rope and a circle of wooden benches.

Marva smiled at an elderly woman at the front desk whom she recognized from her own volunteer trips to the hospital. She had to be ten years older than Marva and appeared to be drifting in and out of sleep. Marva gave her a half-wave, but the woman didn't respond.

Marva pivoted to the right and down the hallway toward the gift shop and the north side entrance. The bright red exit sign became bigger and bigger as she approached; she refused to look in any other direction. When she reached the door she saw something else, something she hadn't seen in Woodbrook in years: snowflakes.

She let go of the IV stand and used both hands to push open the cool, thick glass doors. Then she used her foot to hold it open while she pulled the IV stand outside and then rolled it up against the building. When the door closed behind her, she shut her eyes and slid the IV from her arm. She wanted to wrap the dangling tube around the stand, to make it easier for someone to take care of it later when they found it, but the trip downstairs had used almost every last drop of energy. So she let it hang and float in the air like a drying apron string.

Marva looked at her watch: 5:02. Only then did she realize how cold it was, and she began to shiver. She looked left and then right and was relieved to be alone.

At 5:03 a car squealed around the side of the hospital. It lunged and stopped, then lunged forward again. The engine popped and swore and grunted and the pile of rolling noise came to a final stop in front of a sign marked *No Parking*.

Marva leaned down and looked in the window of the rusty Volkswagen Beetle. "Hi, Zach."

Zach struggled to get the car back in gear while Marva put on the plush cotton robe he'd brought from her home. The car hiccuped and burped its way back through town. Marva prayed aloud when they passed a police cruiser on Main Street and again when Zach stalled the car at the last light before 27 Homes and couldn't get it started again for several minutes.

Finally, with the neighborhood still dark, Zach pulled into the trailer park and down the main road. When they passed his family's trailer, he turned off the engine and coasted the Beetle the rest of the way to Marva's.

He helped Marva up her porch stairs and into her home before giving her a hug and dashing back outside to return the Beetle before anyone woke for Christmas morning. When the car started again on the first crank, he pumped his fist and caught a proud glimpse of himself in the rearview mirror. He turned around in Marva's wide driveway and drove back toward his trailer on the shank. He killed the engine again when he got close, and rolled into the yard. He hopped out with the car still moving and tried to push it back to its exact original position.

He noticed that the snow had picked up slightly, and though it still wasn't sticking, the yard was mushy. He said his own prayer that the snow would eventually cover all of his tracks.

Zach moved carefully through the yard, sidestepping his skateboard and his mother's plastic deck chairs. He took his time opening the back door, pulling it an inch at a time and holding his breath as he stepped inside. He took even more time closing it, careful to hide each unoiled squeak in the otherwise innocent night sounds.

He kicked off his shoes inside the door and tiptoed down the hallway to his room. The door was open a crack, and he nudged it further, finding Charlee asleep on her side and Melvin the monkey watching Zach's every move.

He climbed the ladder to his bunk, crawled under his blanket, and looked up at the ceiling. "Merry Christmas, Charlee," he whispered. "Merry Christmas."

DECEMBER 25

> *On the 12th Day of Christmas*
> *my true love sent to me:*
> *Twelve Drummers Drumming*

Dear Charlee:

At last . . . it's Day 12! Christmas! Did you get something special this year?

We are so excited to share the story behind the Twelve Drummers Drumming. We hope you're hungry!

We should admit that when we first wrote this verse, we truly meant for singers to think of the finest twelve drummers in the land. But then a funny thing happened on the way to 27 Homes . . .

It was just last night, and we were still on a frantic last-minute search. We were so afraid that we wouldn't have any drummers to present to you tonight to represent verse 12.

We were feeling really discouraged when we remembered that nothing fixes the blues like ice cream, right? We drove by Stetter's Ice Cream Parlor. Closed! We swung by Chrissy's Custard. Dark! How about Sandra's Shake Shack? Out of business? Boo!

That left only the frozen food aisle at the grocery store. Not our first choice, but at least there's lots of variety, right?

We wandered the ice cream coolers, but no one in

the family could agree. One wanted plain vanilla, one wanted plain chocolate, one wanted caramel on top, and yet another begged for sprinkles. Soon we were arguing with one another and chasing away the spirit of the holidays.

But then a miracle happened—I stumbled across something I'd never seen before: a box of ice cream treats that had something for everyone. While the rest of the family continued to squabble about what flavor to buy and how many gallons we'd need to please everyone, I snuck up to the register and bought the most glorious assortment of treats I'd ever seen. Something told me this was exactly what we needed to cheer us up and get us ready for tomorrow's final delivery.

I stood in the parking lot with my delicious discovery. One by one my family members found me waiting in the parking lot by the sleigh and apologized for being grouchy. It was clear the search for your twelve drummers drumming had taken quite a toll.

I opened the box of cool confections and handed each of my hungry songwriters the flavor of their choice.

Smiles! Laughter! Dancing taste buds!

After all those years of hunting, after all the rock concerts, marching band competitions, and middle school orchestras, the answer to the Twelve Drummers

Drumming was found in the grocery store right here in Woodbrook!

Sure, these might not be drummers, but wouldn't you rather have the Drumsticks?

Enjoy and share these twelve, tasty frozen treats.

Happy 12th Day of Christmas!
The Traveling Elves

28
Christmas

Charlee wasn't yet awake when the 12th Day delivery landed on the doorstep of their trailer. But by 7:00 A.M., she was up and asking questions.

"Did you see anyone? Did they knock? Can I have one for breakfast?"

She was thrilled when her tired-eyed mother answered the last question with a happy "Absolutely."

Wrapped in a blanket and wearing her favorite knit cap to cover her bald head, she sat on the floor near the tree and ate ice cream while Zach crawled under the tree and distributed the lonely few presents. Both Zach and Charlee got candy-stuffed stockings. Zach's favorite was a bag of old-fashioned creme drops from a company called Zachary Confections. Charlee loved her king-sized Charleston Chew, and she began nibbling on it immediately.

Charlee thought she heard Zach snicker when he opened his first gift, a keychain from their father shaped like Herbie, the Love Bug. Later, Zach opened a gift from Miss Marva: an expensive new video game that Charlee had never heard of, but that would make Zach grin all day long.

Charlee got a gift from Miss Marva, too. It was a beautifully framed photo of the two of them standing in Miss Marva's living room in front of the mantel on Thanksgiving Day. Her Advent calendar peeked at the camera over their shoulders. Charlee was surprised to find a second gift, a bright green apron with two words on the front in white cursive handwriting: *I Believe.*

She put the apron on and Charlee's mother took a photo. "I'll make sure Marva sees this," she said, and her voice snagged on her emotion.

Charlee also opened a gift from Zach, a gold charm bracelet that surprised his parents, too.

"Where did you get that?" Charlee's mother asked.

"I bought it."

"Where?"

"Downtown. After school."

"How?"

"I did some jobs for Miss Marva. She said I'm a really good worker."

"Oh," Emily said, and even to Charlee it seemed her mother felt embarrassed for asking.

Later, her parents insisted everyone eat a real breakfast of pancakes, muffins, eggs, and orange juice. Charlee couldn't remember the last time they'd had such a nice breakfast. "It's like a real buffet!" she said, and no one complained when Charlee drowned her pancakes in so much maple syrup that it dripped off the plate and onto the table.

After breakfast, with Zach's help, Charlee made a slushie with cherry Kool-Aid and snow. Her parents were adamant that she couldn't play outside, but a quick peek in the backyard at the six-inch blanket of fresh white wouldn't hurt. They knew the snow wouldn't last long, and besides, Charlee argued, when had they ever had a white Christmas before?

Standing just outside the back door, Charlee gazed at Miss Marva's house across the field and thought the once green, dandelion-dotted field looked like white clouds. She didn't say it, but she wondered in that moment if heaven's neighborhoods looked like that too.

After breakfast was cleaned up, Zach looked at his watch and announced that he had one final gift. "Everybody back at the table. I have one more thing for Charlee."

"You do?" she asked.

"Yep."

"But I looove the bracelet, Zach." She jingled it from her left arm and felt the charms tickle her wrist.

"Just close your eyes. I'll be right back."

Charlee did, but then opened them again when she heard her bedroom door open down the hall.

Zach whipped his head back around. "I said close 'em!"

This time she put her hands over her eyes to make sure she wasn't tempted to sneak a peek. A minute later, she heard his chair at the table squeak when he sat back down.

"Okay, now say, Merry Christmas."

"Huh?"

"Just say it."

Charlee almost shouted the words, "Merry Christmas!" She anxiously awaited the surprise. It took a moment, and she wanted to open her eyes so badly she began to wriggle and bop up and down.

With her eyes still closed, Charlee heard her mother whisper, "Zach? What's going on?"

"Just wait," he said. "Charlee, say it again."

"Merry Christmas!"

Then, at last, came the scratchy response. "Merry Christmas to you, Charlee."

Charlee's hands flew to her sides and her eyes shot open. She faced Zach's hand, which was holding her walkie-talkie an inch from her lips. "Miss Marva?"

"It's me," she said.

"Are you home?" Charlee shouted, and Zach inched the walkie-talkie away from her mouth.

"I sure am."

"Merry Christmas!" Charlee said again. "When did you get home?"

"Early this morning."

Charlee looked at her mother. "Did you hear that? Miss Marva's home!"

Emily looked at Thomas with the raised-eyebrow-Mom-look that Charlee sometimes noticed, but didn't really understand.

Charlee took the walkie-talkie from her brother and stood up. "It's a miracle!"

There was a long pause before Miss Marva added, "You could certainly say that."

"Are you feeling all right?"

"I'm in bed, and I'm very sleepy, but I'm home. That's all that matters."

Zach gave his sister a fist bump, then stood from the table and eased away, smiling at his parents. When he eventually turned his back, Charlee saw her mother nod in Zack's direction, and her father followed Zach back into their bedroom.

Charlee got up from the table, then laid under a blanket on the floor by the tree and began detailing her Christmas morning. She ran through each gift and thanked her friend for her apron with a giddy gush of enthusiasm.

"I could tell Mom loved it, too."

"You could?"

"Uh-huh," Charlee said, and she sat up and looked to see

if her mother was still in the kitchen. She wasn't, and Charlee whispered, "She cried when I put it on."

"My. That's nice. I'm so glad you liked it."

Charlee described the gold bracelet she'd gotten from Zach and each of the charms. "There's a tiny monkey—it's so cute—a heart, a flower, and a rainbow. He said I can get more charms for it later."

"How nice."

"And he said he did jobs for you."

"That's true. He's been very helpful lately."

Charlee turned over on her back and slid under the branches of the tree. An ornament dangled down and tickled her forehead. "Have you opened the door for Day 25 yet on your calendar?"

"I . . . have," Marva said, though the two words were separated by a cough.

"Oh!" Charlee yelped. "And I got the 12th Day of Christmas gift."

"You did? Already?"

"Uh-huh."

"What was it?"

Charlee jumped up and found the letter. She read it and described the ice cream box and each of the flavors. Then she asked Miss Marva if she knew who Mozart was.

Charlee's questions came faster and faster.

Marva's responses arrived slower and slower.

Eventually she told Charlee she needed to rest for a bit. "We can visit again later, all right, sweetheart?"

"Okay."

"Enjoy the day with your family."

They said good-bye, and every couple of hours she checked in with Marva for a short visit, or to update her on Zach's video game or about the walk her parents took alone, or to tell her about the movie they watched together after a late lunch.

When evening came, Charlee said good night to Marva and set the walkie-talkie on the plastic crate by her bed. And while she was warmly under the covers, her thoughts were across the field.

29
The 13th Day of Christmas

Charlee opened her eyes and was surprised and disappointed to feel so tired. She'd gone to bed early, just like her mom and dad, but when the sun rose, she was still exhausted.

"Good morning," her mother said from the kitchen table. She was writing in her journal and eating a bowl of instant oatmeal. "Feeling good?"

Charlee rubbed her eyes, even though she'd already tried that in her room and it hadn't worked. "Uh-huh. Just tired."

"You overdid it yesterday, didn't you?"

"I dunno," Charlee said, and she slumped into a chair and rested her head on the table, using Melvin as a pillow.

"Stay here," Emily got up and returned with a different thermometer, one the hospital had given them. Charlee liked that it checked for fevers on her forehead instead of under her tongue.

"You're good," her mother said, reading the thermometer and setting it aside. "Lots of sleep today, all right?"

"Uh-huh," Charlee breathed.

Emily finished her oatmeal, put her journal away, and helped Charlee pour a heaping bowl of Cocoa Puffs. "I've got to go to work. You take it nice and slow today, all right?"

"You have to go?"

"I'm sorry, the day after Christmas is very, very busy. I'm already late."

Charlee sat up and rubbed her eyes again. She took off her knit cap and rubbed her head, too. But that didn't shake the cobwebs, either.

"Your dad is in our room, reading. Watch television or play a game. I'm sure Zach will be up soon."

"Okay."

"Don't bother Marva—"

"Miss Marva," Charlee corrected.

"Yes, don't bother Miss Marva before lunch, all right?"

"Uh-huh."

Emily hugged Charlee and kissed the top of her head. "You're beautiful, you know that?"

"Not really."

"But you are."

"Not now, I'm not."

"Of course you are."

Charlee pointed at her bald head, and her mother swiped her hand away, putting both of her own hands on it and rubbing in soft circles. Charlee sighed at the comfort of her mother's touch.

"Hair doesn't make you beautiful, Charlee. *You* make you beautiful."

She kissed her again, shouted "good-bye" to Charlee's dad, and zipped out the door.

Charlee stood and looked out the back window. The blanket of snow remained, but Charlee could hear drips and drops from the trailer's roof, and she knew it wouldn't be long before the field was a brown, melted swamp. She hoped Marva would soon be out of bed and on her feet to see it, too.

Zach slept until 9:30, and then he also moved slowly through his morning routine. Charlee watched television while he ate breakfast, and at 10:00, their father announced he had errands to run and would be gone a few hours.

"Charlee, no walking around the neighborhood, got it?"

"Uh-huh."

"What about me?" Zach said.

"Fine, you can walk, but no driving. She can drive, but no walking. Fair, champ?"

"Ha-ha, Dad," Zach said, and Charlee thought he fake-laughed a little too loudly for the occasion.

Thomas walked out the front door carrying the newspaper and his cell phone bill. "Back soon."

Charlee and Zach played his new video game until he became frustrated, and Charlee suggested they play one of the older games he had already mastered.

At 11:00, Charlee asked, "What time is lunch usually?"

"What do you mean?"

"Mom said I couldn't talk to Miss Marva until lunchtime."

"Lunch is usually at noon for most people, I guess."

Charlee hesitated. "What time do you have lunch?"

"Today?"

"No, at school, on a regular day?"

"Um," Zach looked up at the ceiling as if checking a clock, "I think, 11:20. Yeah, that's when we go for lunch."

Charlee spun and rearranged her knit cap. "I think we eat at 11:45. I think. But I haven't been to school in a while so I don't remember for sure."

The two talked and theorized about lunch times around the world and in various time zones. They suggested that old people, like Miss Marva, always ate earlier, and Zach explained what it meant when restaurants said they had an early-bird special. By the time they were done talking and laughing, Charlee really didn't have to wait until the traditional lunchtime; it was noon.

She skipped into her room for the walkie-talkie. "Good morning, Miss Marva, are you there?"

She did not reply.

"Miss Marva?"

Zach suggested she could be sleeping, or in the shower, or on the phone and unable to answer. Charlee waited a few minutes before Zach nodded and she tried again. "Miss Marva, are you awake? Hello? It's Charlee and Zach."

Charlee set the walkie-talkie on the table in front of her and waited.

Zach walked to the window and looked across the field.

"Hello there." Charlee thought Miss Marva's voice, though low and tired, sounded like an overdue Christmas carol.

"Hello! Are you awake?"

Her response was slow. "Yes, I'm awake."

"How are you today?" Charlee asked.

"Fine, tired but just fine. How are you?"

Charlee got up from the table and went into her room, closing the door behind her and climbing onto her bed. "I'm tired, too. But feeling okay."

There was another long break before Miss Marva said, "Christmas was exciting, wasn't it?"

"Uh-huh. Mom says I overdid it."

"She's right," she said, before another long pause. "Like I always say, she's a smart one. And your father is, too."

"Yeah," Charlee said, and she waited out the silence until she became worried Marva might have fallen asleep again. "Miss Marva?"

"I'm here."

Charlee stood up and walked to her window. "I wish I could see your smile today."

"Me too, Charlee."

The chatter continued until Charlee offered to let Miss Marva rest for a few hours. "I'll check on you later, all right?"

Miss Marva agreed, and the conversation soon died.

At 3 P.M. Charlee tried her again but got no reply. She passed the time by arranging her 12 Days of Christmas gifts along a shelf in her room. She'd even saved the packaging of the ones that were long gone. There wasn't much room, so she packed them in a tight but careful order: the CD of the guy she'd never heard of; two purple gloves; one rolled up, empty paper wrapper that had once held a loaf of French bread; four stuffed birds that made her smile whenever she looked at them, especially at Big Bird; a Krispy Kreme box; six Hawaiian leis; seven small rubber ducks; two of the eight Milk Maid caramels—she'd already eaten six; a stuffed dog named Lady; ten plastic parachute men; eleven kazoos; and an empty variety box of Drumsticks.

At 3:20, she tried Marva again and sang songs to wake her. She sang "Silent Night," then "Joy to the World" and even the revised version of "The 12 Days of Christmas." Nothing worked, so she distracted herself by reading through each of the twelve letters again and making a list of things she still needed to ask her parents about.

At 4:00, Charlee looked through a fat folder of homework the school had sent home weeks earlier. Most of it was easy stuff, and she knew she had lots of time to get it done before going back to school. But she also knew what the adults in her life knew, too. She wouldn't be going back to school anytime soon.

At 4:15, with her mother still at work and her father out running errands, Charlee had finally had enough. She put on her coat, gloves, and her thickest wool cap and woke Zach from a nap on the couch. "Zach, are you awake?" She shook him. "Zach? Are you sleeping? Zaaach. Zach."

"Huh?" he finally said, lifting his head from the couch cushion.

"It's Miss Marva."

"What?"

"She's not answering."

"She's probably asleep. Like I was." Zach rolled over and pretended to snore, exaggerating his breathing and making pig-snorting sounds.

"Very funny, Zach. Come on. I want to check on her."

"Maybe she's gone out. Not home."

"Come on, Zach."

"Try the walkie again," he said, and Charlee pulled on his arm until he sat up.

"No, I want to really see her."

"Charlee," Zach said, and Charlee thought he lowered his

eyes just like an adult would. "You know you can't walk over there. You promised Dad."

"I know, I know, I know." Charlee smiled. "But *you* can."

Zach walked very slowly across the backyard. "You okay up there?"

"Yep, keep walking." Charlee clung to Zach's shoulders and Melvin the monkey clung to hers.

"You know we're going to get busted," Zach said. "Look at the prints in the snow."

"Just keep walking. There's only one set."

Zach stepped through the fallen fence and nearly tripped.

"Don't drop me!" Charlee said.

The closer they got to Miss Marva's house, the more excited Charlee became. "Hurry, Zach."

"I'm not a horse, Charlee."

"So what?" she said. "You can be one today." Charlee pulled on his shoulders like reins. She couldn't wait another minute to be inside Marva's house. She hadn't visited her friend in her own home since Thanksgiving—since the day everyone's life had changed. "Come on. Hurry, Zach."

He didn't let her feet hit the ground until they'd arrived at the back porch. They both knocked, but no one came.

"Miss Marva?" Charlee shouted through the closed window. "Miss Marva?"

No response.

"Now what?" Charlee asked.

"This." Zach pulled a house key from his jeans pocket. He unlocked and opened the door. "Come in. But be quiet."

They entered through the kitchen. "Miss Marva? Are you home?"

They stopped in the living room, and Zach put his arms on Charlee's shoulders. "Wait here."

Charlee looked around the room. Even with the tree and some of the other decorations on loan in her own home across the field, Miss Marva's house still appeared to have been the model for a holiday gift catalogue. Charlee looked at the Advent calendar and noticed that the doors for the first twenty-five days were open, but empty. The unusual door marked "26," however, was still closed. She walked toward it and reached for the golden star knob when she noticed a white envelope sitting flat next to the calendar, blending in with the decorative white cotton fabric.

Charlee picked it up and found her name scrawled on the front in small, cursive handwriting. She opened the envelope and removed a single piece of stationery with a red bow and silver bell border.

—————— ❄ ——————

DECEMBER 26

On the 13th Day of Christmas
my true love sent to me
the most valuable gift of all:
FAITH

Dear Charlee:

It's here! The 13th Day of Christmas has finally arrived.

I'm so happy that you're home for the big occasion. I have been praying for you, and I will continue to pray for you in this life and the next. That's what we do for the people we love.

I hope you've enjoyed the first 12 Days of Christmas and the quirky twist on the song. I know who's been writing the letters, but I am sworn to secrecy. I'll confess that I might have given them the idea, but that's it.

I will also confess that I shared the idea on the condition that I got to write the final verse. It only seems fair, right?

I don't mind if the Traveling Elves remain a mystery forever, that's up to them. But I wanted you to know exactly where Day 13 came from, because it's the most important day of all.

Charlee, I also want you to know that this isn't my first year with the 13 Days of Christmas. Long ago my husband used to write these fun stories for a different family every year. We started the year after our son, J.R., died, but when John also passed away, I just couldn't carry on the tradition without him.

Sometimes we chose a family with a very special need. Maybe it was a lonely widow. Or someone fighting sickness, like you, or sadness, or both.

I remember one year when John chose a family who didn't seem to need anything at all. They looked to have everything you could ever want. But something told John that they needed the experience. I think he was right.

Every year was a little different, and the Traveling Elves always had a twist on where each verse of the song came from. John was such a storyteller. Your dad reminds me of him.

Of course, we had the very same deal. John wrote the first twelve days, with my help when he needed it, and I also helped with the gifts to go along with the verses. But the 13th Day was always mine to write.

I'm so happy that I get to write this 13th Day of Christmas to you, Charlee Alexander. I said that it wasn't my first, but it's probably my last. I could not think of anyone I'd rather share the 13th Day with more than you.

The others have been so fun, haven't they? They've lifted your spirits, and mine, too! They have been silly, unbelievable tales to put some magic in the days that led to Christmas.

But today, Charlee, this 13th Day of Christmas, isn't about donuts, caramels, or plastic parachuting men. It's more than that.

It's sacred.

I know you're young and that word—sacred—and

this letter will not mean the same today that it will mean next year, or the year after, or even when you're old and saying good-bye, like me. So don't you worry that it doesn't all make sense yet, sweet Charlee. In time, it will. The letter will grow with you, and everyone you share it with.

So what is the 13th Day of Christmas? Why does it come on December 26th?

It's actually quite simple, Charlee. The world spends all year racing to Christmas, racing to gifts, trees, lights, and treats. These are good things, they are important traditions, and they add color and meaning to the season. Just like the first 12 Days, that shiny side of Christmas is something to cherish.

But if that's all we have, we're missing something, Charlee, aren't we? We're missing the most valuable lesson of all. What good is remembering His birth if we don't remember His life? His birth wasn't the end. It was the beginning!

Charlee, I know it's been a difficult year for you in many ways. And I also know that it's not over yet and that challenges still remain.

But please know, Charlee, that Heavenly Father and His Son love you. I know this is true. I know they are aware of you. They know your needs and hear your prayers.

My! How they are proud of you! You've met your trials with faith and hope!

This Christmas, I wish for your family to know that there is a plan for you, a way Home, and it starts with how all of us live our lives on December 26th.

Charlee, the greatest gift I have is knowing that He is waiting for me. If I die today, I know He will be there. But I don't have to see Him to know that.

Finally, Charlee, please remember that on the good days and the bad days, you are loved.

When your family is upset or when there isn't enough money, or food, or hugs, you are loved.

He wants you to know that.

And I want you to know that, too.

Charlee, this is the 13th Day of Christmas.

> *Love forever,*
> *Miss Marva*

P.S.: Next Christmas, there is something waiting for you behind the last door on the Advent calendar. It is my most prized possession, and I want you to have it.

Charlee carefully returned the letter to its envelope and stared at her name on the front. Behind her, Zach's footsteps began as a soft, off-rhythm drumbeat and became louder and steadier as he moved up the hallway. She turned to face him when the sound stopped, and when she saw Zach's cheeks, drenched with tears, she knew Miss Marva Ferguson was living the 13th Day of Christmas with Him.

30
One Year Later

Charlee crouched behind the overgrown bushes that supported the mailbox. She held an envelope marked *The 1st Day of Christmas* and a fountain pen made from a turkey feather. Inside the envelope, a letter explained that the feather was actually from a partridge, and that an invisible pear tree would be delivered overnight.

No one had ever come clean about last year's 13 Days of Christmas, but when Charlee asked her mother, Emily had pinkie-sworn that she'd had nothing to do with it. So Charlee suspected the men in her life, led by her father, had somehow pulled it off. Once, when she asked new family friend, Rusty Cleveland, if he knew anything about it, he zipped his lips shut and changed the subject.

Charlee already knew that Marva had planted the idea, of

course, and had asked to remain at a distance. She'd provided money and moral support for the gifts, but Charlee believed she'd not read a single letter before delivery. It tickled her to know that when Charlee read them over their walkie-talkies, Marva was really hearing them for the first and only time.

The Alexanders were proud to carry on the tradition, writing new, whimsical letters and leaving them each night for the lone remaining porch waver who still lived on the bend in 27 Homes. Her two dear friends had died earlier that year, and her loneliness was as clear as the two empty chairs on either side of her.

Night by night, beginning on December 14, Zach and Charlie would leave the letters and gifts on her porch, knock, and then race each other down the street and into the darkness. When the coast was clear, they would glide through the night, past the trailer that used to be theirs, and into their new home.

Even then, months after everything had been finalized, Charlee still couldn't believe that Miss Marva's house was theirs. Marva had left Rusty her prized Miata and his choice of aprons from her collection. She'd also left a small cash gift for the Woodbrook Library and the Woodbrook Mercy Hospital. A handful of Miss Marva's volunteer friends were given their choice of aprons, too. Each had tearfully sorted through the pegs and hooks and picked one that had special meaning.

Despite her best intentions to pay tribute to Miss Marva's

clothesline memories, Charlee's mother soon purchased a new washer and dryer. But in a nod to their generous friend, the family continued to wash Miss Marva's aprons by hand and hang them on the clothesline that stood as a memorial.

Miss Marva had been buried by her husband at a cemetery on the other side of Woodbrook. Charlee and her family visited occasionally, but they all agreed they felt closer to her when they stood at the clothesline in the fresh air and hung her aprons to dry by the hand of heaven.

Miss Marva had another surprise. Not only had she left the home mortgage-free to Charlee and her family, she'd also secretly arranged for every nickel of Charlee's bills at the hospital to be paid for as long as she needed treatment. One year had passed since her diagnosis, and Charlee was cancer free.

Charlee and her family knew it could return anytime, anyplace. They'd seen the numbers, understood the risks, and had attended three funerals that year for other children who'd lost their own battles. But Charlee also knew that if she died one day, if she met God face-to-face, her faith in Him wouldn't be any stronger than it already was.

On December 26, Charlee would share that faith on a piece of paper and deliver it. She would testify that while Christmas was important, the most divine day of the year was the day after.

The day to recommit to living a life more like His.

The day to proclaim to the world that while His birth brought hope, His life brought the model.

The day to believe that He lives, that He loves everyone, and that He wants every porch waver, rock pile climber, cancer patient, and troublemaker to come Home again.

The 13th Day of Christmas.

EPILOGUE
December 26

Charlee had hardly slept. Yes, Christmas Day had been exciting. It was everything Charlee had ever dreamed of in their new home. They'd gotten a few gifts, had dinner with Rusty, and secretly delivered the 12th Day of Christmas gift without any hiccups.

Still, as wonderful as the day had been, Charlee couldn't wait to jump from bed and open the final day on the Advent calendar that hadn't moved from the mantel all year. She'd been tempted to open it many times since Miss Marva's death, to peek inside and see what magic—seen or unseen awaited—but she'd honored her best friend's wish that she wait.

Charlee also couldn't wait to pass along the magic of Day 13. She knew that opening the small red door would unlock the day and usher in the reminder of what it all meant. She didn't know exactly what she'd find, if anything at all, but she knew Miss Marva would be watching.

Charlee tiptoed down the hallway from her bedroom in the dawn light. She walked through the living room to the pantry and picked an apron for the morning, just the way Marva would have. She went with one of Marva's favorites. In curly cursive, a screen-printed message on the front of the apron boasted *If life gives you lemons, throw them through the candy shop window and grab some taffy.*

The apron made her smile.

She inched into the living room and approached the mantel reverently, like a child at a church altar. Charlee paused a minute, took a deep breath, and pulled the golden knob on the only closed door on the calendar: 26.

Instead of an empty tomb, she found a faded, folded piece of white paper. It was creased four times so it would fit in the calendar's small compartment.

Charlee opened it and recognized Miss Marva's handwriting in the upper right-hand corner. She'd scribbled the words *Received on December 26, 1970.*

Charlee sat on the couch and read the letter for the first of many times in her life. When she was done, she retrieved Miss Marva's letter about the 13th Day of Christmas and read it again.

And with each new year, as she passed from girl to teen to woman, she read both letters often, and she discovered that

Miss Marva was right: the letter's rich meaning grew right alongside her.

Dear Mom and Dad,

It's been too long since you've gotten a letter. I apologize for that. It's been a difficult month here. I hope you get this before Christmas, but I guess it doesn't really matter.

I'd wanted to write all last week, but I couldn't find the time or a quiet place. It's early morning, and I'm writing this from the trees, not far from the front. We're camped on the edge of a green field, and the fog is lifting from it like it's afraid of the day.

Lately I have learned something about myself. I think losing a few guys has really changed me.

It took a while—a long while—but I'm not afraid to fight anymore, and I think it's made me a better soldier. I'm also not afraid to die, and that's made me a much better man.

Sometimes I see you guys in everything. The sky, the jungle, the faces of my friends. But I know that even though I cannot see you, you're still there.

I've never really thought of it before, but isn't that what you taught me about God? I've never seen Him, but I know He's there.

Who knows what awaits me today, or any day. I

want you to know that if I don't make it across this field, if I am to see God tonight, He will be no more real than He is right now.

I wish I could send you a gift, something special to open on Christmas. One day I'll hug you both and maybe that will be a gift to all of us, right? Until then, I guess this letter is my gift to you.

Mom and Dad, because of you, I believe in God.

Because it's Christmas, I've been thinking more than usual about what you taught me, about how God sent His Son to be born in a manger, to live, to teach, to die, and to be born again, resurrected, for us. I know that's true.

I've been thinking how I used to count down to the big day. We would try so hard to think of Jesus, but we knew the traps. We knew that the meaning of Christmas can become lost in the ripped wrapping paper on the floor.

So we try to remember Him. On Christmas Eve, Dad would read His story from Luke in the New Testament. We felt good about ourselves that we'd worked so hard to remember that Christmas is about the birth of Jesus.

Then what?

On December 26th, we return the clothes that didn't fit, and we begin to put Christmas back in the box. In the basement. Or by the curb. We mark the day off the calendar and prepare for the next holiday and the chance to ring in the New Year. What a shame that the day after

Christmas just might be the least memorable day of the year.

I've learned that it doesn't matter how I'm living my life today, or tomorrow, or on Christmas Day, or how much I remember Him and His birth, if I don't wake up a different man on December 26.

Isn't that what He wants?

Not to simply celebrate Jesus' birth on one day, but to celebrate His life by living like Him the other 364?

Do we worship the infant for a day, but not the man and His teachings all year long?

Do we put Him away with the decorations?

Or do we try to be more like Him?

That's my Christmas gift to you. I hope you get this by Christmas, but if you don't, think of me on the day after.

Now that I've reread this letter, I'd say December 26 might be my new favorite day of the year. I guess you could call that the 13th Day of Christmas.

Please enjoy my gift. It's the most valuable thing I have: December 26th.

Love,

J.R.

Author's Note

In my family, the tradition of the 12 Days of Christmas has a long history. As children, my siblings and I watched our father conjure up incredible stories of mysterious elves doing good for those in need. Each story was accompanied by a clever gift and left in secret on the target's doorstep. The stories were never the same year to year, and the gifts ranged from the obvious to the absurd. Some took a few minutes to assemble; others took hours.

The concept of the 13th Day was not part of our family tradition, but I think if my father were alive today, this is exactly where the tradition would have evolved. He had extraordinary faith in Christ, and he knew that the gifts and stories were fun, but that the only true and lasting joy of the holiday came from living a life more like the Savior's.

You may feel inspired to write your own fun, whimsical verses and leave gifts with a family in need this holiday season. If you're so inclined, please visit www.the13thdayofchristmas.com for suggestions, templates, and other free information that might help you.

If you choose not to embark on the full 13 Days project, please consider sharing the simple 13th Day concept this year with people in your life. In a note, perhaps you might share what the day means to you and the essence of your personal faith. In a troubled world, testifying of Him and His love for each of us is the most valuable gift you can give this Christmas, and it's a gift that grows the more we give it.

Leave your note by itself on a doorstep or in a mailbox or accompanied with your favorite holiday treat. Better still, look the recipient of your 13th Day gift in the eye and hand your note to them with a heartfelt expression of love.

Finally, never forget that He stands ready to carry your burdens, if you only let Him.

Happy 13th Day of Christmas.
Jason Wright

On the 13th Day of Christmas: